For the Good of the Cause

For the Good of the Cause

Seán Damer

www.stridentpublishing.co.uk

Published by
Strident Publishing Ltd
22 Strathwhillan Drive
The Orchard
Hairmyres
East Kilbride
G75 8GT

Tel: +44 (0)1355 220588
info@stridentpublishing.co.uk
www.stridentpublishing.co.uk

Cover art by Susan Pierce Sloan
Cover design by Lawrence Mann (LawrenceMann.co.uk)

A catalogue record for this book is available from the British Library.

ISBN 978-1-905537-62-4

Typeset in Palatino by Andrew Forteath | Printed by Bell & Bain

The publisher acknowledges support from Creative Scotland towards the publication of this title.

For my old friend and compañero
Andy Pollak,
remembering the craic, the good times in the hills,
the encouragement to write a novel,
and – Biggles and the Belfast Brigade!
¡Venceremos!

The Outer Hebrides

and the Isle of Skye

PREFACE

On July 22nd 1745, Prince Charles Edward Stuart landed on the island of Eriskay in the Scottish Outer Hebrides from a French ship. He had come to regain the British throne for his father, James Stuart, the "Old Pretender," who lived in a small palace in Rome in exile as King James III of Scotland and VIII of England. His Jacobite supporters called him "the King over the water;" the term "Jacobite" came from the Latin for James: "Jacobus". The Hanoverians who actually ruled the United Kingdom called the Prince the "Young Pretender". He raised the Jacobite standard at Glenfinnan and some, but not all, of the clans in the Highlands and Islands, and some Lowland towns, rallied to his support. For example, major clans like the MacDonalds of Clanranald and the MacDonalds of Sleat did not come out for the Prince, and instead were mustered into the Highland Militia, a form of pro-government Territorial Army. However, many of the officers and men of this Militia were secretly sympathetic to the Jacobite Cause.

After a series of spectacular early victories, and marching into England as far as Derby, the Jacobite army retreated back into Scotland, and suffered a crushing defeat at the Battle of Culloden on April 16th, 1746. The Prince went on the run, aided by loyal clansmen, and pursued by the "Redcoats," the regular soldiers of the British Army. If he had been captured, he would have been executed summarily. We know this because of the fate of the young Jacobite officer Roderick Mackenzie, who was the very double of the Prince. The Redcoats surrounded him at Glen Moriston; Roderick drew his broadsword, and the Redcoats shot him on the spot. As he fell mortally wounded, he cried, "You have murdered your Prince". Following several close shaves, the Prince reached the island of Benbecula in the Outer Hebrides on the night of April $26^{th}/27^{th}$.

The Hanoverians soon learned that the Prince was hiding on the neighbouring island of South Uist, and organised a massive manhunt for him, involving both Redcoats and the Highland Militia. This hunt was led by Captain Caroline Scott of the Army, and Captain John Ferguson of the Royal Navy, both men with a terrible reputation for merciless cruelty. In the meantime, the French had sent Neil MacEachainn, a South Uistman who had served in the French Army, to the Outer Hebrides, to orchestrate the escape of the Prince on a French warship.

Twenty-three-year-old Flora MacDonald was in South Uist where her step-father, Captain Hugh MacDonald – one of those officers sympathetic to the Jacobite cause – was in command of the Highland Militia. She was herself no Jacobite. However, when the exhausted Prince was guided to the family shieling in the middle of the night by Neil, Flora's sense of Highland hospitality rose to the occasion. With the help of her step-father, she famously arranged the escape of the Prince over the sea to Skye. Thus, Flora was a heroine who had heroism thrust upon her.

Chapter 1

My early childhood in South Uist was very happy. My own father had died when I was barely one year old, but to be perfectly honest, I have no memory of him at all. So Marion, my mother, my brothers Ranald and Angus and I did everything together. Every night at bedtime, Mother would tell us one of the old stories, or sing one of the *sean nos*, the old traditional Gaelic ballads, and in that way we learned of our history and culture. Mind you, we worked hard too, for we had the two farms at Milton and Balivanich to run. But I enjoyed making butter and crowdie, and waulking tweed with the women; in short, I was a happy wee girl.

All of that changed when I was six. One night, Captain Hugh MacDonald came over from Skye in a boat for my mother. There were armed men in the boat, and a piper, who played a march as the Captain took my mother down to the boat while our servants screamed their heads off. It was scary, because I didn't know what was going on, but I noticed that Mother was all dressed up and laughing, and the Captain had a great big grin on his face. I called out to my mother, but she said she'd be back in a few days, and the servants would look after us children. I was frightened as I watched that boat sail off into the night. Where was my mother going?

Mother did come back in a few days, with the

Captain. She called us children in, and told us that Captain Hugh MacDonald was now her husband, and our stepfather; MacDonald of Sleat had given his permission for the marriage. I was black affronted, stamped my foot, and insisted that the Captain wasn't my real father. He said he knew that, but if I gave him a chance, he would be as good a father to us as he knew how.

That night, Mother did not come to the bedroom as usual to sing us a song. Ranald and Angus soon fell asleep. But not me. I slipped out of bed and tiptoed down the stairs to her bedroom; she would always let me snuggle up to her in bed while she told me a story. I could hear the murmur of Mother and the Captain talking inside. She laughed out loud, then gasped. I tried the door handle; it was locked! It had never, ever been locked before. I tiptoed back upstairs, slid into bed, covered my head with the blankets, turned my head to the wall and sobbed myself to sleep. My mother had betrayed me to a man with – with only one eye – who had stolen my mother from me.

I vowed I would never let anyone see that I was hurt by this betrayal; oh no. What I did was become an impassive and self-controlled girl; nobody ever knew how I was feeling or what I was thinking. I was always polite and attentive to mother, but avoided my step-father as much as possible. There were no complaints or recriminations; I just got on with whatever I was asked to do.

As I grew older, all of this had effects, of course, although I wasn't aware of it at the time. When they reached about fourteen or fifteen, most of the other local girls became interested in boys, and were always talking about getting married. But boys didn't seem interested in me. By the time most of the girls were twenty, they were married, but I wasn't, and anyway, I didn't think I was pretty, although I had a nice complexion unmarred by smallpox. It would have been nice to have married and have had a baby, but it didn't look like it was going to happen. Apart from anything else, most of the young men were scared of my step-father.

However, I did enjoy the company of the women in our community, and still waulked tweed with them, sang our Gaelic songs, listened to the stories of our ancestors, and danced at ceilidhs. Sometimes I sensed that the older women felt sorry for me for some reason, but I could always find an inner peace by walking on the machair and in the hills; our island has great beauty.

But to tell you the truth, Captain Hugh proved as good as his word, and was an attentive and loving father to us children, and a good husband to Mother. It was also plain that he had a bright future in Clan Donald, for he told us that the Chief of Sleat wanted him to be his Factor in Skye. But then, in 1745, when I was twenty-three, the Jacobite commotion started.

Chapter 2

Milton, South Uist, Outer Hebrides,
Summer 1746.

The Highlands and Islands had been awash with rumours of a rising for months. The rightful King of Scotland, James Stuart, was in exile in Rome with his son Prince Charles Edward, while Britain was ruled by the Hanoverian usurper, George II. Secret agents from France came and went, and government spies were everywhere. I knew that my stepfather, Captain Hugh MacDonald, was up to something because strange men arrived in the middle of the night. My stepfather had been an officer in a Scottish regiment in the French Army and had lost his eye in a battle; he was a famous warrior, a great swordsman, and like all Scotsmen in the French Army, a Jacobite.

Local fishermen reported seeing French ships in the Minch. But when Prince Charles Edward Stuart landed on Eriskay in July of 1745, he came alone; the promised French army did not materialise. This put the clans on the islands in a terrible dilemma: whether or not to come out for the Prince. The chiefs of Clan Donald in the islands – MacDonald of Sleat in Skye, and Old MacDonald of Clanranald in South Uist – refused to bring out their men. Instead, they were mustered into the Highland Militia, which supported the Hanoverian government; my stepfather was put in charge of the Militia in South Uist. Disappointed, the Prince went on to Moidart, where he was joined by Young Clanranald with several hundred of his men from the mainland, and Cameron of Locheil with his men. They raised the Stuart standard at Glenfinnan.

But I can reveal that quite a few local men slipped away and joined the Prince. My brothers Ranald and Angus wanted to go, but my stepfather wouldn't hear of it, and they joined the Militia. So the situation was very complicated; clans were divided, as were families within clans, for and against the Prince, and you had to keep your wits about you and your mouth shut. You never knew who was on which side.

We heard the news of the Prince's progress, of course, his victory over the Redcoats at Prestonpans, his taking of Edinburgh and marching into England. But still the Chiefs on the islands didn't call their clans out. Then when the Jacobite Army turned back at Derby, my father said it would soon be all over.

"The government in London will bring the Regular Army back from the Continent, and force the Jacobites into a set-piece battle they cannot win," he said. And he was right. The Hanoverians faced the Jacobites at Culloden, and as we all know, the result was a catastrophic defeat for the rebels. The government in London exacted a terrible revenge all over the Highlands, and I heard stories of wholesale killing, rape and burning from the fugitives who made it back to the islands.

***

My mother decided to have a ceilidh for the Militia officers and locals to take our minds off the terrible news from the mainland. I was excited because I love our music, and like to dance. We had two fiddlers, a piper with the small pipes, and a bodhran player; everyone is the area was invited, so there was quite a crowd.

I moved round with a tray of drams of *uisge beatha,* whisky, and glasses of claret. The young men of the village were gathered in a corner, and I offered them drams. They were polite enough towards me, and I knew them all well, of course, for we had gone to school together. But I caught them glancing over their shoulder at Captain Hugh; they were afraid of his reputation, you see. This worried me a bit, for I didn't want them to be so scared they wouldn't ask me to dance. In fact, my step-father's reputation as a warrior was such that I had not really been courted yet, which was embarrassing to tell you the truth. But my parents seemed to think that none of the local lads were good enough for me. Lachlan MacNeil smiled at me.

"It's a grand gathering right enough, Flora," he said. "You've done well."

"Thank you, Lachlan," I said. I knew he liked me, and I liked him. It was an open secret that his older brother, Donald, had crossed to the mainland and joined the Prince's army. But there had been no news of him for weeks; his family feared the worst.

Just then my father announced an Eightsome Reel and I was delighted when Lachlan asked me to dance. As we whirled round, I saw my Mother and Step-Father smiling as they clapped time, so they must have approved of Lachlan. And I saw old

Coinneach MacDonald grinning and muttering in his wife Mairi's ear; matching-making, no doubt.

When the dance came to an end, I was going to take the drinks round again, but Mother asked me to sing a song. My father called for silence, and there was an immediate hush. I decided to sing the Gaelic song, '*Tha mi am chadal, na duisgibh mi*' – 'I am asleep, don't waken me.'

I am grieved at the struggle
Which has outlawed every clan -
I am asleep, don't wake me up;
Without joy, without happiness,
Without any settlement from [King] George -
I am asleep, don't wake me up.
There is many a lady
Who is now lonely in her bed-chamber,
Without joy, without happiness,
Rising all alone:
Mourning forever the gentlemen
Whose hands they won in marriage –
I am asleep, don't wake me up.

Alas for the young men
Who were not lacking in courage,
I am asleep, don't wake me up;
In time of sword-unsheathing,
And in time of blow-striking,
I am asleep, don't wake me up.
Though now you are scattered
Among the glens and hills,
You will rise again

When it is time for you once more to be heroes:
Until James comes across
And your swords become bloodied,
I am asleep, don't wake me up.
He is king of the pigs
And King of the Whigs, King George -
I am asleep, don't wake me up;
Until Hallowtide comes round,
And until his neck is in ropes,
I am sleep, don't wake me up.
But if you would arise
With hardihood and manliness,
Both vassals and nobles,
Tenantry and peasantry,
And if you would sweep him away,
The foreign king who does not belong to us,
I would happily sleep with you.

As I sang, there was absolute silence. Everyone in the room knew the meaning of the song, even although the island was plastered with posters offering thirty thousand pounds for Prince Charles Edward Stuart, the "Young Pretender," dead or alive. And many people present were related to a man in the Jacobite Army, and were praying for his safe return. So it wasn't surprising that there was a storm of applause when I finished.

Chapter 3

The next day was lovely, the kind of cloudless summer weather you can get in the Hebrides. As I strolled along the machair singing to myself, the sun was warm on my skin, the breeze ruffled the wild flowers, the sea sparkled, swallows swerved past me, and a noisy flight of oystercatchers fed at the waterline. Thank God, it had been dry for weeks, so there were very few midges about. Away to the east, the peaks of the Cuillin Hills in Skye were etched in purple. Out to sea in the Little Minch, a British Navy warship headed for Lochboisdale with all sail set. I wondered what its mission was; whatever it was, it wouldn't be good news.

Half-a-dozen wee girls were skipping in the sun, singing the chorus of an old song I knew well.

Far am bi mi fhìn is ann o bhios mo dhòchas
Far am bi mi fhìn is ann o bhios mo dhòchas
Far am bi mi fhìn is ann o bhios mo dhòchas
Far am bi mi fhìn bidh mo dhòchas ann.

"Hello, Flora," the girls chorused.

"Hello, girls," I said. "So it's *Far am bi fhìn* you're singing. Caw the rope and I'll jump in."

The girls swung the rope, I jumped in, and we all sang the verse.

Siubhal air na cladaichean 's a' coiseachd air a'ghainmhich
Siubhal air na cladaichean 's a' coiseachd air a' ghainmhich
Siubhal air na cladaichean 's a' coiseachd air a' ghainmhich
Far am bi mi fhìn bidh mo dhòchas ann.

Laughing, I jumped out. "Och, I think I'm a bit too old for this. Cheerio, girls."

"Cheerio, Flora."

I continued along the machair, so wrapped up in my thoughts that I started when old Coinneach spoke.

"Ciamar a tha thu, a' Floraidh mo ghraidh?" he said – How are you, Flora my dear?

I smiled at the old man, who was carrying a creel full of herring. He was one of my father's most trusted tacksmen, and I knew he had been out in the 1715 Rising and fought at the Battle of Sheriffmuir with Old Clanranald. He was a sprightly fellow who didn't look his seventy years.

"Och Coinneach," I said. *"Tha mi gu math."* I'm well. "I was day-dreaming."

"It's a grand day for it," said Coinneach.

I gestured at his creel. "You've had a good catch then."

"Aye, the silver darlings are running well. Here, take these for your mother and father." He gave me half-a-dozen herring, which I placed in my apron.

"I'll be off, then, Flora," Coinneach said. "Mairi will be waiting to grill the fish for our tea. *Chi mi a-rithist thu.*"

"Yes, I'll see you later," I said. "And thanks for the herring."

The old man waved and set off for the village, his

creel on his shoulder. It was then that I saw something out of the corner of my eye, out on the moor. I squinted into the sun and saw a kilted figure approaching at a stumbling run; he was vaguely familiar. As I watched, he collapsed, and lay without moving. I dropped the herring and ran towards him. When I reached him, he was gasping for breath, filthy, unshaven, with red-rimmed staring eyes, and a grimy and bloody bandage tied round his head. At first I recoiled, but then recognised him.

"Donald MacNeil," I said. "My God, man, what happened to you?"

His eyes rolled as he gasped, "After Culloden... everywhere, Flora, in the Highlands...it's a massacre...burning and killing...everywhere..." He fainted. I ran all the way to the village, caught up with old Coinneach, and told him about Donald. He glanced around, shoved the creel into my arms, and said, "Give this to Mairi, and don't tell a soul what you've just told me." He then whistled up a couple of neighbours, and they set off at a run.

I don't know what happened next and I don't want to. But Donald MacNeil vanished, I didn't see him for well over a year, then met him in Skye. By then, he was healed and well, but leaving for America. His last words were to thank me for fetching help for him.

Chapter 4

Mother, Father, my two brothers and I sat at the table, the men all in the uniform of the Highland Militia. Morag, our servant, placed a roast joint of venison on the table, then a bowl of potatoes. Father poured the claret, said "*Slainte mhor!*" and we set to.

"Is there any news of the Prince's whereabouts, Father?" Ranald said.

My stepfather glanced about. "He's supposed to be on the Long Island as we speak," he said. That meant he could be anywhere from the Butt of Lewis to Barra.

"How on earth will he get away?" Angus said.

"There's talk of French ships in the Minch," Ranald said.

"There's always talk of the French," Father said. "Just like the French army which never arrived."

"Well, Morag's father saw a French frigate while out fishing," Mother said.

"Aye, aye," Father said. "How could he be sure – "

Outside, there was the sound of raised voices, then a cry from Morag. The dining-room door burst open, and in stalked a Redcoat officer. He was a stout man, with the coldest eyes I have ever seen, and a face red from drink. My stepfather was just about to explode with rage when the Redcoat spoke.

"Captain MacDonald, I presume?"

"I am," Father said. "And who the devil – ?"

"I am Captain Caroline Scott of His Majesty's Sixth Regiment of Foot, sir," said the Redcoat. "And I am the Officer Commanding all government forces here on Uist. *All* government forces. Including the Highland Militia."

I glimpsed Mother put her hand on Father's knee under the table to restrain him, for he was fizzing with fury. Captain Scott continued.

"As of tonight, there is a dusk to dawn curfew on South Uist, until we find the son of the Pretender. Kindly call out this...this Militia of yours, sir, and enforce the curfew forthwith. Anyone breaking the curfew is to be arrested and brought to me personally. Anyone. Understood?"

As I feared my stepfather would explode, I stood up.

"Captain. You must be exhausted after all your travelling," I said. "May I offer you some refreshment?"

"My step-daughter, Captain Scott," Father said. "Miss Flora MacDonald."

"Charmed, I'm sure," Scott said, sitting down. "A glass of wine would be most acceptable, Miss MacDonald."

As I poured him a glass of claret, Father carved some slices of venison, while Mother said, "*Ceud mìle fàilte gu mo dhachaidh, a' Chaiptean.*"

Scott said, "I don't have the Erse, Madam."

So I translated for him. "My mother says, a hundred thousand welcomes to my home, Captain."

I knew that a lot of Sassenachs called our Gaelic "Erse", or "Irish"; it was just another way of insulting us.

Father placed the venison on a plate and handed it to Scott, smiled, and said, *"Tha mi an duil gun tachd e thu"* – I hope it chokes you. Then Father said, "That's our Gaelic for 'Bon appetit,' Captain."

We all managed to conceal our grins as the Redcoat officer ate.

Chapter 5

That night, I was awakened by something, some noise from outside. I got out of bed, put on a gown and peered out of the window. Tendrils of cloud raced past a full moon. Then I saw a figure flit out of the barn towards the house. A moment later, there was a squeak from the front door. I opened my bedroom door a crack, heard urgent whispering from downstairs, and saw the flicker of a candle. I tiptoed down the stairs; a stair creaked, the whispering stopped immediately, and there was a scuffle of feet. I paused at the dining-room door; there was a lit candle on the table.

"Father, is that you?" I said.

I stepped into the room. Suddenly, a hand clamped over my mouth, and a dirk was held to my throat.

"Neil! It's Flora," Father said.

The hand released me, and I staggered back, terrified out of my wits. A figure stepped into the candlelight from behind the door, dirk in hand. It was a kilted man armed with broadsword and pistols; he sheathed the dirk.

"Flora, it's alright," Father said. "This is Neil MacEachainn of Howbeg."

"*The* Neil MacEachainn?" I said. "But, but, I, I thought you were in France."

"I was," Neil said. "But now I'm back home again. I'm sorry to have frightened you, Flora. And I am very pleased to meet you."

"Flora, Dear," Father said. "Bring some victuals for Neil. He's had a long hard journey."

A little later, in the light of several candles, I watched as Neil wolfed a makeshift meal of bread, cheese and cold venison. As I poured him a glass of claret, I studied him covertly. So this was the famous Neil MacEachainn. I had heard he'd gone to the Scots College in Paris, but didn't have a vocation for the priesthood, so joined the Royal Scots regiment of the French Army. Many of our young men did this. But there were also rumours he was some kind of secret agent for the French, and had been seen on the Long Island before the Rising. Mind you, they were only rumours.

Neil was an athletic, clean-shaven man, maybe five foot eight inches, with a broad chest and shoulders. As my father would say, 'he looked to be a good man in a tight corner.' I myself thought his eyes were incredibly beautiful, and shone with an intelligence far beyond his years. He had a handsome, mobile face, and an air of self-confidence and strength about him. He drained his glass and I poured him more wine.

"Thank you, Flora," he said. He looked at Father. "So as I was saying, that's my mission."

Father nodded knowingly, and scratched his chin as if to say: it's a difficult one. I glanced from one man to the other, wondering what this mission was. Then Father indicated me with a jerk of his head, and an interrogative wrinkle of his brow. Neil glanced at me, then looked away. He shook his head briefly in the negative. But my stepfather nodded yes, there's no other way. I was completely baffled, and hurt that, whatever it was, Neil didn't want me involved.

"Would someone mind telling – ?" I said.

"Flora," Father said.

"Yes, Father?"

"Flora, my dear. Tomorrow, I want you to take the cattle up to our shieling at Unasary. Coinneach will go with you."

"Unasary? But – " I said.

"That's a good girl, Flora," Father said. "Go back to bed now. It's late."

As I climbed the stairs, my mind was racing. There was definitely something funny going on, but I hadn't a clue what it was all about.

Chapter 6

The next morning, as Coinneach and I drove the cattle up Sheaval Hill towards Unasary, my mind turned to my stepfather, for Eusdan Cam was an impressive man in anybody's book. The Jacobite commotion made life difficult for us on the Hebrides. Although Clan Donald on Skye and the Long Island had not come out for the Prince, and it staffed the Hanoverian Highland Militia, the fact of the matter was that the vast majority of local MacDonalds were sympathetic to the Stuart Cause. Although he seldom said anything about it, I knew that my stepfather was too. But other local clans like the MacLeods were not, so we had to be careful, very careful. I knew something was in the air, but couldn't make out what it was.

"Look, Flora," Coinneach said.

Below us, a Royal Navy man-o'-war rounded the point.

"Sassenach bastards," Coinneach said.

The crew let the wind out of the ship's sails, and the roar of the anchor-chain through the hawsepipe could be heard clearly if faintly. As we watched, two longboats were lowered, and Redcoats clambered down a scrambling-net into them. We turned away and drove the cattle on.

"Away you go down, Coinneach," I said. "It's not far to the shieling now. I can manage fine on my own.

Off you go."

"Right you are," he said, and set off down the hill towards his croft.

***

As the cattle grazed peacefully, I washed my hands and face in a barrel of rainwater. It was a tranquil evening, with grand views over the whole of South Uist, and still very light, as the summer nights are out here on the islands. As I took in the view, the Northern Lights flickered and flashed; the 'Fairy Dancers' we called them. I smiled at the thought, yawned and took myself off to the shieling.

I was in the middle of a dream – about dancing with Lachlan MacNeil – when I was woken by a noise outside. I froze, listening. There it was again: a faint chink of metal. My body went rigid; there was someone at the door. The door opened an inch, then stopped. I could hear fast shallow breathing. Suddenly, the door swung open and a figure bounded into the room, covering every corner, a pistol in one hand and a broadsword in the other. A shaft of moonlight illuminated his face. It was Neil MacEachainn.

"Neil! Man alive!" I said. "What a fright you gave me."

"I'm sorry, Flora," he said. "Get up and get dressed. I need your help."

He turned with his back to me, uncocked his pistol and sheathed his broadsword. I stumbled out of bed, put on a petticoat and gown, lit a couple of candles, and blew the smouldering embers of the peat fire into life.

"Right, I'm ready," I said. "What is it, Neil?"

"I have the Prince outside."

I gasped, and my hand flew to my mouth. "Oh my God! Here in Uist?"

"Aye," Neil said. "He's up the hill. He's in a bad way, Flora. I need your help."

"Have you gone quite mad, Neil MacEachainn?" I said. "Why on earth did you bring him here? The Redcoats are all over the place. If they find out the Prince is here, they'll burn every last house on the island and kill every last man."

"I know," Neil said. "But – "

"But nothing. You've got to get him away from here. At once."

"Flora. Please. It's too dangerous. It, it was your father's idea to bring Himself up here. That's why he sent you up in the first place."

My jaw dropped; now I understood all the mystery. Then, behind Neil, a wraith of mist swirled through the door, and a figure stepped into the candlelight. There was no mistaking him; it was the Prince. He looked remarkably like the picture on the "WANTED" posters: he was a tall man, perhaps five foot ten inches, fair-skinned with a long face, wearing a travel-stained kilt and carrying a knapsack. He looked exhausted, but carried himself erect. He looked at me, with disdain, I swear.

"Why am I left waiting outside, sir?" he said. "And who is this, this female?"

"Elle est des notres, monseigneur," Neil said.

I understood that alright; she's one of us.

"Ah, voila," the Prince said. "Qui est-ce, cette jeune femme?"

"May I present Miss Flora MacDonald, the daughter of Captain Hugh MacDonald of Milton, whom you met at Moidart?" Neil said. "Flora, his Royal Highness, Prince Charles Edward Stuart."

I was absolutely speechless. I didn't know that Father had met the Prince at Moidart. Then I remembered my manners, and curtsied. The Prince bowed.

"Mademoiselle," he said. "I am pleased to meet the daughter of such a loyal and devoted servant."

"Why, Sire," I said, "thank you."

I took in the Prince's appearance. His clothes were worn and dirty, his eyes were red with fatigue, he was unshaven and badly sun-burned, covered with scabby midge-bites, and had a gash above one knee which was leaking blood.

"Och, the *truaghan,*" I murmured. "Would you look at the state of him?"

"Mademoiselle?" the Prince said – then fainted and collapsed in a graceful heap on the floor.

"Oh my God," I said, and rushed forward. Neil helped me lift the Prince onto a chair; he came to with a groan.

"Madonna mia," he said. "What happened? I feel quite light-headed."

"He hasn't eaten since the day before yesterday," Neil said.

"For pity's sake," I said.

I grabbed a pewter tankard from the table, filled it with cream from the coggie and gave it to the Prince.

"Here, sire," I said. "Drink this. It will do you good."

He gulped it down, then looked up at me, his lip smeared with cream. "Have you anything to eat?"

I grabbed a dirk and cut slices of bread and cheese. As I did so, the Prince took a small canteen of silver cutlery out of his knapsack, and set himself a formal place at the table. I glanced at Neil in astonishment; he shrugged in an embarrassed manner as if to explain that it was what Princes did.

I put the food on a pewter plate and passed it to Himself. He wolfed it down, taking swigs of milk. I put out another plate of bread and cheese for Neil, then snapped my fingers as I remembered the claret. I filled a large glass and passed it to the Prince. He toasted me silently, drank a mouthful, and sighed with pleasure. Neil was still standing. So, puzzled, I gestured him to the table.

"What are you waiting for?" I said. "Sit down and eat, man."

Neil shifted his feet, but the Prince said, "Asseyez vous, je vous en prie."

Neil sat and ate. I took in the Prince's nearly bare legs below his kilt; they were covered with scratches, septic and still leaking blood. So I poked the peat fire, filled a pot with water from the rain-barrel, hung it from the crane and swung it over the heat. We had to get this man sorted out.

"If you would lift your foot, sire," I said.

The Prince lifted his right foot, I untied his brogue and took it off, then gently unrolled his hose, which smelled pretty ripe. I hid my disgust, but recoiled when I saw a louse crawling down his bare leg. I picked it up and threw it in the fire, then gently washed his foot, then his lower leg. The Prince closed his eyes and sighed with pleasure.

I felt Neil's gaze upon me, and turned to glance at him. His eyes were fixed on me, and, I swear, were glowing. He smiled encouragement, and I don't know why, I blushed and turned back to my task. I tapped the other leg, the Prince lifted his foot, I removed his brogue and hose, and washed that leg too. Then I studied the gash above his knee.

"That's a nasty cut," I said.

I stood up, emptied the basin out of the door, and refilled it with hot water from the pot. Kneeling down, I cleaned the gash as gently as I knew how, but the Prince winced and groaned. I stopped for a second, then continued to clean the wound; I could feel the Prince trembling with pain.

"Neil," I said. "Would you get me a handful of sphagnum moss from the bog?"

As Neil went out of the door, I rose to my feet and picked up a small hip-flask of whisky from a shelf. I poured some onto a clean rag, and dabbed at the wound. The Prince groaned again.

"I'm sorry," I said.

"Pray continue, mademoiselle."

Neil returned with the sphagnum moss. What I needed now was a bandage. I glanced around the shieling, but couldn't see anything that would do. So I stood up, lifted my petticoat without thinking, tore a strip off the bottom, and caught Neil gazing at my bare legs. Embarrassed, he looked away. I tore the strip of cloth in half, knelt down again, and bandaged the Prince's wound. Then I took the moss from Neil, packed it on top of the bandage, and gently but firmly tied it in place with the second strip of cloth.

"There," I said. "That should do it."

I stood, looked at Neil, then back at the Prince. Outside, the sun was up. "I suggest that you rest for a while, sire."

"Yes, I will," the Prince said. "I am exhausted, if the truth be told."

Neil and I helped him onto the bed, pulled the plaid over him, and he went out like a light. I turned to face Neil.

"The *truaghan,*" I said. "The poor man. We have to help him. Now I understand why you came back from France."

Chapter 7

Later that day, having conferred with Neil, I hurried down the hill from the shieling, but stopped dead when I spotted a column of dark smoke rising vertically into the air. From a bluff, I saw red flames licking out of the thatch of Coinneach's cottage away below. Outside, a group of Redcoats milled about in a circle, shoving someone backwards-and-forwards. I set off downhill again at a breakneck run.

When I reached the cottage moments later, it was fully ablaze, and I saw that it was a badly beaten Coinneach whom the half-dozen Redcoats were pushing about. The soldiers were all drunk, passing a large jar of whisky around.

"Mairi," Coinneach cried.

I sprinted towards the Redcoats, and yelled, "Let that man be!" The soldiers stopped and turned towards me. Coinneach collapsed.

A Redcoat staggered towards me, saying in a foul Cockney accent, "Well, well, well, what 'ave we here, lads. A fine Highland wench wot – "

I pushed him aside, saying, "Stand back, soldier."

Kneeling beside Coinneach, I wiped the blood from his face with my petticoat; I could see he was dying. The Redcoat advanced towards me again, fumbling at his flies.

"Come on, lads," he slurred. "Let's have a bit of fun wiv this 'ighland bitch."

Coinneach grasped my hand, and gasped in Gaelic, "Mairi. Inside. In the house…." He groaned, and died in my arms. I stared at him for a moment, then closed his eyes and laid him on the ground just as the Redcoat grabbed my shoulder.

"Right, you 'ighland bitch, I'll – "

But a Corporal said, "No, leave 'er alone, Perce. She's trouble, that one. I reckon she's a lady or somefink."

The Redcoat stepped back, muttering obscenities. I stood up, ran to the door of the burning cottage, and cried, "Mairi!"

The Redcoats chanted, "Mary. Oh Mary. Where are you?"

"Don't fink Mary's good for much now, mates, eh?" the Corporal said.

The Redcoats staggered off, howling with drunken laughter, passing the whisky jar about. As acrid smoke billowed out of the door and flames roared out of the thatch, I pulled the skirt of my dress over my mouth and dashed inside.

Moments later, I stumbled out, retching and crying, eyes wide with horror, fell to my knees, and vomited violently. Behind me, the blazing thatch of the cottage collapsed with a crash.

***

I burst through our dining-room door to find my stepfather sitting in a wing-chair with a glass in his hand.

"Father, Father," I cried. "The Redcoats have

murdered Coinneach and Mairi. And they – "

Father stood, and said, *"Bi séimh, a' Floraidh, bi séimh."* Calm yourself, Flora, calm yourself.

"Did you not hear what – ?"

Father took my hands in his, his eyes signalling caution. "Shush, girl."

I realised there was someone else in the room. I spun round to see Captain Scott rising from his chair; he half-bowed.

"We meet again, Miss MacDonald," he said.

"Why? Why did you do it?" I said.

"Do what, Madam?"

"Your, your men murdered old Coinneach and Mairi MacDonald. For no reason."

"Murdered? I would hardly believe so, Madam. My men would not act without reason."

"Without reason? Your men were drunk. A harmless old couple. You, you should have been there to stop them."

"Madam. I am sure you will allow that I cannot be in two places at the one time."

"Your soldiers were utterly out of control, sir. And, and violating Mairi was an outrage. An, an old woman."

"I do regret the local, ah, commotion, Madam. But my orders are from the Duke of Cumberland himself. A rebel is a rebel, Miss MacDonald. The only good rebel is, therefore, a dead rebel. So whenever we find a rebel, we execute him. Or her. Whatever the circumstances. These are the Duke's express orders. We intend to extirpate these damned Jacobites once and for all."

I glared at Scott for a couple of moments. "And how do you know who is a Jacobite, sir?

Scott laughed. "We know, Miss MacDonald, we know. Have no fear about that. And when we find the last of them, the Young Pretender – "He ran his forefinger along his throat. "Why! There will be no more Jacobites. The whole kingdom will be safe for the House of Hanover. Forever."

Father took my arm. "You must excuse my daughter, Captain Scott," he said. "She is distraught."

"Quite so," Scott said. "Quite so. But then, young ladies have no place in a theatre of war."

Chapter 8

I watched from behind the curtains at my bedroom window: Redcoats everywhere. Half-a-dozen cavalry trotted past, scattering villagers. They bowled a child over, and her screaming mother ran to pick her up and console her. The cavalry sealed off the entrance and exit to the township. A Redcoat foot patrol directed by Captain Scott on a black horse kicked the doors of the houses in, and searched them, turning the furniture over. An extended line of Redcoats appeared over the skyline, sweeping the village. I looked down; a couple of Redcoats stood at our front gate. They saw me, looked right up at me, and said something very nasty. Where was Father?

I had to do something quickly. To make an impression on the Redcoats, I dressed smartly. Over my white linen shift, I put on a red-and-white striped linen petticoat, a green wool skirt and jacket, a striped apron, hand-knitted woollen stockings, and shoes with one-inch heels. Then I tied a pale blue silk ribbon round my hair, and completed my outfit with a tartan arisaid, fastening the plaid at my breast with a silver buckle. I looked at myself in the mirror; that would do the trick.

Picking up a basket, I took a deep breath and sailed out of the front door. The two Redcoats at the gate blocked my way. I recognised one of them as the Corporal who had been at Coinneach and Mairi's cottage. With a leer, he said, "Sorry, Miss, our orders are – "

"I am Miss Flora MacDonald," I said, "daughter of Captain Hugh MacDonald, the Officer Commanding the Highland Militia on South Uist, and I do not take orders from Corporals." I swept past them; you should have seen their faces.

Our hayshed appeared to have been searched; there were no Redcoats at this end of the townland. Glancing about, I slipped inside, and whispered, "Neil! Psst!"

Neil's face appeared from the straw at the top of the shed, right under the roof.

"Come quickly!" I said. "The Redcoats have gone."

Pistol in hand, Neil slid down from the top of the pile, followed by the Prince. I glanced out of the door and said, "Right, follow me."

We darted down the lane to the inn; the searching Redcoats could be glimpsed in the distance. The inn door opened a crack, and old Ceit MacLellan beckoned.

"Flora! This way," she said. "They've been here already."

I slipped inside, followed by Neil and the Prince. The inn had been turned over, with tables on their sides, stools upside down, and broken bottles everywhere. Ceit showed us through to the back door, and I peeked out; all clear. Suddenly, Neil swore under his breath. I turned and saw the Prince, a happy smile on his face, pouring himself a glass of brandy from an unbroken bottle. Pistol in hand, Neil grabbed him by the arm and pulled him towards the door, the glass going flying.

We jinked up the hillside above the townland and hid in a pile of boulders from where we had a good view; it was very hot. In the distance, a line of Redcoats vanished over the skyline. I was panting for breath and sweating with all my good clothes on, while the Prince waved a stalk of bracken in a vain effort to keep the midges away, muttering what sounded like very bad words in Italian.

"We can't keep this up for much longer, Neil," I said.

"I know," Neil said, frowning. "Wait, I've an idea. I'll take Himself over the hill to Corrodale. My brother was gamekeeper there, and there's a bothy. There's no path in, and you can't see the bothy from the sea. So he'll be safe until we decide what to do next. Go back and tell your father. Ask him to arrange for supplies to be sent in. Just walk slowly, act natural, and you'll be fine."

He squeezed my shoulder encouragingly, and smiled. I smiled back, and set off down the hill, feeling strangely happy.

Chapter 9

As I breasted the hill overlooking Corrodale, leading the pack-horse, drunken singing wafted up to me. Down below, I could see the Prince, my brother Angus, Old Clanranald, Lochboisdale and MacDonald of Baleshare beside the burn. They waved glasses about, the Prince clutched a bottle of brandy, and they bellowed some French drinking song.

"Chevalier de la table ronde,
Goutons voir si le vin est bon.
Goutons voir, oui oui oui,
Goutons voir, non non non,
Goutons voir si le vin est bon."

Neil lay just below the skyline, telescope and weapons at hand, his face showing his disgust. He jumped to his feet when he saw me and helped pull the laden pony into the shade; it was so hot that the air shimmered. I sat on a boulder, took a mouthful of water, and looked down at the drinkers; the sight was hard to credit. Five grown men drinking themselves senseless when there was a manhunt on for the Prince, and thirty thousand pounds on his head! I turned to Neil.

"Does Himself always drink as much?" I said.

"Oh aye," Neil said. "That man drinks a bottle of

brandy a day without even thinking about it."

"Good Lord. How do you put up with it?"

"With great difficulty." Neil spat into the heather. I glanced at him, admiring his stoicism. Neil clicked his telescope open and scanned the landscape; nothing moved in the heat.

"I'll have to get down with the supplies," I said.

"I'll be here when you get back," Neil said with a grin.

Down at the grassy patch beside the burn, I tethered the pony and unloaded the supplies that Lady Clanranald and Lady Boisdale had given me. There were clean shirts and hose, a tartan coat, plaids, a silver drinking cup, bread, cheese, venison, newspapers, money and yet more brandy. Not one of the men came to give me a hand.

"My Lady Flora," the Prince said, "pray come and join us in some refreshment."

"Sire," I replied, "it is not seemly for a lady to be drinking. And I wish to be back at Milton before nightfall to hear what the Redcoats are up to. Good day to you."

The drinkers chorused a drunken farewell, and I glared at Angus as I left, leading the pony. The Prince was already opening another bottle of brandy.

Back up at the col, I stopped to chat with Neil. As we sat in the sun, he told me all about going to the Scots College in Paris as a boy, but although successful enough at his studies, he had decided that the priesthood was not for him, and had left to join the *Royal Écossais* regiment of the French Army.

"So you speak French?" I said.

"Oui. Je parle Français," Neil said.

"My, my. And, and are the girls in Paris very pretty?"

Neil laughed. "Pretty? They are indeed. But..."

"But?"

"They are not as pretty as the girls in South Uist."

"Go on with you," I said, feeling my cheeks burn.

"No," Neil said. "Nowhere near as pretty." He put his hand on mine; it was warm. He gazed into my eyes. I looked down; Neil put a finger under my chin and lifted it up. I stared at his lips. As his head moved closer to mine, I could feel his warm breath on my cheek. My heart started to beat like mad. Suddenly, there was a bellow from below.

"Mon cher MacEachainn!" the Prince roared.

Neil jumped to his feet. "Monseigneur?" he shouted.

"Venez boire un coup avec nous."

"Non, merci. Il faut que quelqu'un reste comme sentinelle qui n'est pas ivre."

Neil sat down again. "*Drongaire!*" he muttered.

"What was all that about?" I said.

"Himself wants me to go down and have a drink with them. But I told him we've got to have a lookout who is sober."

I stood up. "I have to go, Neil," I said. "Father will be waiting for me with news of what the Redcoats are doing."

"You'll let me know?"

"Of course. Take care of yourself, Neil."

"Aye. You too, Flora. You too."

Going down the hill, I thought if I turned round

and he was still looking, it would mean he thought me pretty. Turning, I looked back. Neil was silhouetted on the skyline, watching. I waved; he waved back, and vanished. The rest of the journey home seemed to pass in seconds, I was so happy.

Chapter 10

The next morning, I came downstairs to find Father in urgent consultation with a mud-splattered Ranald, who had just ridden hard down from Benbecula.

"That's the situation, Father," Ranald said. "And I have to get right back to my men."

Ranald gave me a quick hug, ran outside, vaulted onto his horse and was off north again at a gallop.

"Ah, there you are, Flora," said Father. "I need you to do something for me. Urgently."

"What is it, Father?" I said.

"Get over to Corrodale at once, and tell Neil that General Campbell has ordered Captain Scott to sweep the whole of South Uist from north to south. They've already started. They must know Himself is here. We've got to get him off the island to somewhere safe. Tell Neil to outflank the cordon to the east, and I'll think of something. We need to get Himself over to the mainland where the French can pick him up from a sea-loch. It's becoming too hot here."

" 'Outflank to the east', Father?"

"Yes. Neil will know what I mean. Off you go, as quickly as possible. I'll get another messenger to Neil as soon as I have more intelligence on what Scott is doing. In the meantime, I'll spread a wee story…"

***

As I sat outside the bothy gasping for breath, Neil fetched me a beaker of water. The Prince watched open-mouthed, for I had positively flown down that hill.

"Captain Scott and his Redcoats are scouring the whole of the island from north to south, coast to coast," I said. "He'll be here in a day or two. Father says you are to outflank him to the east while we come up with a plan to get the Prince over to the mainland. It's too dangerous here now. The Redcoats must know Himself is on the island."

"Have you a plan, my lady?" the Prince said.

"Not yet, sire," I said. "But I will."

***

Captain Hugh MacDonald and his son Alan, both in their Highland Militia officers' uniforms, strode down the village street. The minister, the Reverend MacAulay, a weasel-faced man, appeared and made a beeline for them.

"Good day to you, minister," said Hugh.

"Good day, Captain. Still on the hunt for the Pretender?" the minister said.

"Aye, we are that. We've scoured the island for him. But I fear he's given us the slip."

"And where do you think he would have gone?" the minister said. "Lewis – or Harris, maybe?"

Hugh glanced around, and leaned close to the minister's ear. "Between thee and me, a wee bird said he's gone to St. Kilda."

"St. Kilda?" the minister said. Hugh nodded. The

minister scurried off. Hugh and Alan exchanged a knowing look, and continued on their way.

***

"I have an idea," I said.

"What's that, Flora?" Neil said.

"I have a perfect excuse to be travelling to Skye. I could say I was only visiting my father and brothers here, and what with all the harrying of the people by the Redcoats, my mother will be worried sick back at Armadale. So I have a legitimate reason for travelling."

"Aye," Neil said. "And?"

"Well," I said. "If we could spirit Himself over the sea to Skye somehow, he would be safe with the Chief of Sleat, my kinsman."

"Yes," said Neil. "He didn't bring his clan out, but he would still protect Himself secretly, and – "

"And it would be easier for a French ship to reach him there, or in Knoydart, or Morar."

The Prince interjected. "But how would you take me to Skye, my lady Flora?"

"Sire," Neil said. "Flora's father is in command of the local Militia companies, as you know. He therefore has the authority to issue her with a passport permitting such a journey."

Neil turned to me. " But, Flora, his Royal Highness is too distinctive a figure, and the posters with his description are everywhere. How would we get him over the Minch undetected? The English navy patrols it day and night."

"I grant you, that is a real problem," I said. "It would be very risky. Hmm." I snapped my fingers. "But it would be less risky if the Prince did not travel as the Prince."

"I don't follow you," Neil said.

"The Redcoats and the Skye Militia are looking for a man," I said. "We could send a, a woman."

"A woman?" Neil said.

"Aye," I said. "We could disguise the Prince as a woman."

The Prince snorted. "A woman? What a ridiculous idea."

"Aye," I said. "Could you organise a boat, Neil?"

"I could. And a trusty crew. But who would the Prince be?"

"Em, my maid," I said. "An, an Irishwoman, I think. Um, Betty. Yes. Betty Burke."

"A maid? A servant woman?" the Prince said. "I fear you are joking, Mademoiselle."

"Sire, I assure you I have never been more serious."

"I have never heard a more preposterous suggestion in my life," the Prince said. "That my royal personage should be disguised as a servant, and a servant woman at that!"

"Sire," I said, breathing deeply to control my rising anger. "I am a woman and I am serving you. Desperate times require desperate measures. Have you a better idea?"

"Well, I, that is, em – no. No, I do not." The Prince got up and stormed off in a rage, lashing out furiously at the midges, and cursing and swearing in Italian under his breath.

I turned to Neil, and spoke in Gaelic. "Neil, I will obtain a passport from my father and take the Prince to Skye. As my maid. And you will come, as my man, to protect us two defenceless ladies in these troubled times."

Neil laughed, patted my shoulder, and let his hand rest there. I liked that; it was reassuring. "You are some woman, Flora MacDonald. I will be your man any time you want."

I smiled back, and placed my hand over his. "And you are some man, Neil MacEachainn. I will be your lady any time *you* want." I squeezed his fingers.

A flash of a secret shared crossed Neil's face.

"Now, while I go and see Lady Clanranald about clothing and supplies, you skulk up the east coast with Himself, and organise the boat. I'll send a shepherd boy to find you in a day or two."

"Right, Flora," Neil said. "It's a risky plan, but we have no other."

"Who dares not put it to the touch, to win or lose it all," I replied.

Neil nodded, and drew me closer to him. Just then, the Prince stalked up, and we dropped our hands and stood apart.

"Well, then," the Prince said. "When does the masquerade commence?"

Chapter 11

As I hurried up the road to the Benbecula ford, my mind was a whirl; I couldn't get Neil out of my head. He was the first man I had ever met who treated me as an equal. All the young men in Uist talked to me rather cautiously, giving the impression they feared I might bite them. I knew what is was, of course; there were enough men on the islands who had served with my stepfather in the French Army to be wary of him. It was natural that Father and Mother wanted a good marriage for me; I could understand that. But to get married, I had to be courted first and that wasn't really happening, to my secret embarrassment. There were a couple of young men who liked me; I knew that intuitively. There were Lachlan MacNeil and Alan MacDonald, for example. But they hadn't made a definite move.

Neil was different. He talked to me like a grown woman, consulted me about every move to do with the Prince, and when he thought I wasn't looking, his eyes followed me. On the couple of occasions when his hand had touched me, I could feel real warmth, and something more than that, a, a current of energy flowing between us. He was an attractive man in a quiet sort of a way, but with a glint in his eye. He didn't talk about himself much, but I had a feeling that he was just as deadly as my stepfather in his own way. I felt safe with Neil around, and liked his company. It was just too bad that –

"Halt!" the Redcoat Corporal said, startling me so much that I gasped out loud, and froze on the spot.

I was in the narrow track down to the ford, with high banks on either side. Several Redcoats appeared; they were the very soldiers who had been guarding our house. The Corporal grabbed my arm, and squeezed it viciously.

"Well, well, well," he said. "It's the Militia Captain's daughter wot don't take orders from Corporals, innit? And where are you going to, my pretty maid?"

"That is none of your business," I said.

"Oh but it is, petal. Come along wiv you." He pulled me none too gently down the track to the ferryman's house. I must say I loathed his revolting Cockney accent; it was like a pig with laryngitis talking English.

A large bonfire blazed on the shore at the entrance to the ford, and several Highland Militiamen warmed their hands. As we approached, I recognised some of their faces in the glow of the fire, and started singing in Gaelic – *port-à-beul,* we call it – 'mouth music' in English; the words can be nonsense, for skipping songs, for example, or to accompany waulking the tweed. But this time, they were not nonsense.

"Faigh m'athair," I sang, *"Gu grad."*

Go for my father. Immediately.

The Militiamen got it at once. Without looking at me, and still warming his hands at the fire, one of them sang in tune, "Right, Flora."

"Shut your mouf, you 'ighland bitch!" the Corporal said. He opened the door of an outside storehouse, and shoved me in; he slammed the door and rammed the bolt home. I heard him say, "Nick up to the big 'ouse, Perce, and tell Captain Scott we've got a prisoner." My blood ran cold.

I looked around the storehouse; it was full of the ferryman's gear for his boat – sails, oars, rope, rowlocks. I put my ear to the door; there didn't appear to be anyone outside. So my hands flew over the gear, looking for some implement. I selected a rowlock, and inserted it in the crack of the door; it just fitted. So I wiggled it backwards and forwards, trying to move the bolt. There was a promising squeak, and the bolt moved a fraction. Just as I was applying pressure, I heard footsteps approaching. I tossed the rowlock aside, and took several deep breaths.

The bolt was drawn and the door creaked open. Captain Scott stood in the doorway, a glass in his hand, swaying slightly; I could smell the liquor off his breath. He looked me slowly up and down, then advanced into the storehouse pulling the door to behind him.

"Well, Miss MacDonald," Scott said. "We meet again."

My blood turned to ice-water and my flesh crawled, but drawing myself erect, I said, "By what authority am I detained in this place, sir?"

"By my authority, Miss MacDonald. I am the authority in these parts. You were caught attempting to cross the ford at nightfall."

" 'Caught', sir?" I said. "I was about to cross the ford on my lawful business."

Scott advanced slowly towards me; I backed away,

but was brought up short by a pile of sails. "And what was that lawful business, pray?" he said.

"I was on my way to see Lady Clanranald at Nunton, sir."

"I see. On what precise business?"

" 'Precise business', sir? I have no need of precise business. Lady Clanranald is my kinswoman."

"Indeed. So she is. So is everyone on this damned island, it would appear."

Scott drained his glass, and threw it over his shoulder; it shattered on the ground and I started.

"Yes," he said. "The ever-so-polite and ever-so-cool Miss MacDonald. But I'm sure you're really quite warm underneath it all." As he leered at my bosom, I pulled myself together.

"I demand to see the Commanding Officer immediately," I said.

"Hark at the lady. She demands to see the Commanding Officer. Well, madam, *I* am the Commanding Officer, and my word is – "

"No it is not, " I said. "And forbye, sir, you may be an officer, but assuredly you are no gentleman."

Scott snarled, swung his open hand back to slap me, when I heard feet approaching rapidly. Scott dropped his hand and stepped back. The door swung open, and there was Father, his right arm across his body, his hand grasping the hilt of his broadsword. He glanced from me to Scott and back.

"Are you all right, girl?" he said in Gaelic. "Did he touch you?"

I had to think quickly. If I told Father what I thought was going to happen, he would kill the

Redcoat on the spot. Then all Hell would break loose. Scott's sickly face showed that he knew it too.

"No, Father," I said. "I'm fine."

Father studied my face for a moment, then turned to Scott.

"Sir," he said. "I heard that my daughter had been arrested for breaking the curfew. But that was unintentional. She forgot to take the state of the tide into consideration, the silly girl. With your permission, I'll pack her off to Lady Clanranald's directly. That should keep her out of trouble."

Scott swallowed, and said, "I think that would be an excellent idea, Captain MacDonald. We wouldn't want to see Miss Flora in any trouble."

Chapter 12

Lady Clanranald, Lady Boisdale and I sewed up the Prince's clothes. Lady Clanranald worked on a flowered calico gown, Lady Boisdale on a quilted petticoat, and I sewed flounces onto a linen bonnet because it was vital to hide as much of the Prince's face as possible. As we worked, I listened to the ladies' chatter with some astonishment. They bombarded me with questions about the Prince, what he looked like, what he wore, and what he said. They told me they would give anything to be in my shoes, attending to the Prince; little did they know!

I was to meet this strange fascination with the Prince again later, with Lady Bruce and Lady Mary Cochrane in Edinburgh, and Lady Primrose in London. By that time, I had begun to understand that the allure was the whole romantic notion of the Jacobite *cause*. The idea that the Prince himself might be a tiresome bother never even entered their head; how could it? These ladies never met the man, never had to deal with his bad temper, drinking or irresponsible behaviour. So I answered their questions blandly, and what I didn't know I made up. But I never mentioned Neil's role in the whole affair; it seemed prudent not to discuss him at all amongst women who talked so much.

There was a clatter of hooves outside. I rose, looked

out of the window and saw Father dismount. He came in, greeted the ladies, and asked for pen and paper, saying that he was going to write out a passport for me. He sat at an escritoire, and for several moments there was the sound of his pen scrinching over paper, as we sewed away.

"That should do it," he said. "I've framed it as a letter to your mother in Skye. Here's what I've said." We stopped sewing and listened. Father cleared his throat and read:

> *"My dear Marion,*
> *I have sent your daughter away from this country lest she be in any way frightened with the troops lying here. She has got one Betty Burke with her, an Irish girl, who she tells me is a good spinster. If her spinning please you, you may keep her till she spins all your lint; or if you have any wool to spin, you may employ her. I have sent Neil MacEachainn along with your daughter and Betty Burke to take care of them.*
> *I am*
> *Your dutiful husband*
> *Hugh MacDonald.*
> *Captain."*

I nodded. "That is capital, Father. That should do us fine."

Father folded the letter, put it in an envelope and gave it to me.

"You will have to excuse me, ladies," he said. "But the search for the Young Pretender goes on." As he left, he winked at me.

Shortly afterwards, the clothes were ready. We made a parcel of them, and Lady Clanranald added a pair of hooped stockings, a pair of lady's shoes and some clean shirts. Then she put a couple of bottles of brandy and some victuals in a saddlebag. It was then I remembered.

"Good Lord," I said. "I've clean forgotten something. The Prince's face is covered with stubble. If he is to pass as a woman, he must be clean-shaven. What will we do?"

"I know," Lady Clanranald said. "I'll put in some of my husband's shaving tackle."

She vanished and reappeared with a flat-ground razor, a cake of soap and a horn comb which she put in the saddlebag.

"Now his Royal Highness can look like a fresh-faced Irish colleen," she said, laughing.

Chapter 13

At first, I couldn't find the bothy where the Prince was hiding. I scoured the moor on my pony in the area Neil had told me about, but couldn't see it. I actually smelled it before I saw it; I smelled the peat fire. It was a typical low bothy, the stone walls covered with lichen, and heather growing in the thatched roof; perfect natural camouflage. I opened the door, let my eyes adjust to the gloom and stepped down onto the earth floor. A peat fire smouldered in the centre, the smoke making its way out through the thatch. The Prince lay asleep beside the fire, wrapped in a plaid; there was no sign of Neil. So much for security, I thought.

I coughed; the Prince woke with a start. "Mademoiselle?" he said.

"Where is Neil, sire?" I said.

"He is attending to the boat for Skye, and will be back directly. What have you there?"

"I have your women's clothes, sire. And some clean shirts, supplies, and brandy from Lady Clanranald."

"Capital, capital. Pray let me have a bottle of brandy directly."

"Later, sire," I said. "The island is teeming with Redcoats, and I have to attend to your disguise immediately. I am sure we will leave as soon as Neil has organised the boat."

"Confound the Redcoats. I wish to refresh myself

forthwith."

"No, sire. First of all, I would like you to step outside and shave. I have a razor and soap for you. You must remember that you are supposed to be a woman. And women do not have beards, in Scotland at least."

To my surprise, the Prince guffawed with laughter. "Very good, mademoiselle, very good." I held the door open and he went outside.

I took the razor, soap and comb out of the saddlebag as the Prince sat on a boulder. Just as I was about to hand them to him, he stuck his chin in the air and said, "Pray proceed, Lady Flora."

I gaped at him in astonishment; did he really think I was going to shave him? He did; he did indeed. I realised that he had probably never shaved himself in his life, but would have valets or whatever they were called who would dress and shave him.

"Sire," I said. "I have never shaved anyone in my life."

The Prince looked at me in astonishment. "Really? Never? Just soap my face and scrape it off with the razor, my dear lady. That's all there is to it."

I took off my arisaid, rolled up my sleeves, filled a pannikin with water, and rubbed the soap in it until I had worked up a lather, which I then massaged into the Prince's face with my fingertips. His eyes shut, the Prince murmured, "You have gentle fingers, Lady Flora."

I then picked up the razor, and with my tongue between my teeth, began to shave the Prince. As I scraped away, I got the hang of it. In a few minutes,

I finished, asked the Prince to rinse his face, and handed him the comb. Just then, Neil returned. The Prince greeted him, saying, "My Lady Flora makes an excellent barber, Neil."

Neil couldn't hide the look of astonishment on his face. His eyes signalled: did you actually shave him? Suppressing a smile, I nodded. Neil grinned, then said, "We have a boat, sire, crewed by reliable men, all from the Highland Militia."

"Good," I said. "Then let us dress the Prince."

I handed the Prince the gown, petticoat, shoes and stockings, and he said, "What will I do with my kilt?"

"Keep it on under the petticoat, sire," I said. "We may have to abandon the women's clothes in a hurry."

But the Prince fooled about, striking poses, and pulling up the gown to expose his stockinged legs. I gave him the bonnet, and he tried to push the flounces back from his face, muttering with exasperation under his breath. He wasn't the only one who was exasperated. I knocked away his hand and re-arranged the bonnet, saying, "Pray do not touch the bonnet, sire. The flounces are meant to hide your face."

The Prince then picked up his pistol, and raising his gown and petticoat, made to hide it. I grabbed it but the Prince resisted, so I slapped his hand sharply and removed the pistol.

"No pistols, sire," I said. "If you were searched and the pistol found, it would give you away directly."

It was then I noticed the astonished look on Neil's face; he obviously thought it was *lèse-majesté* to slap the Prince's hand. When he saw me glaring at him, he gulped and glanced away.

The Prince smirked and said, "My dear lady, if we should happen to meet with anyone who would search me so thoroughly, why, I am sure they would soon feel the prick."

Neil gasped and turned away in mortal embarrassment. I had had enough of the Prince's clowning, and now foul mouth, so when I spoke, I spoke with icy emphasis.

"The point, sire" I said, "is to prevent any more killing. There has been quite enough on your account already."

It was the Prince's turn to be embarrassed; he averted his eyes. Neil was just about to say something conciliatory when I saw young Rory, the local shepherd boy, streaking through the heather towards us.

"Redcoats! Redcoats!" Rory said. "Coming this way!"

"Quick, Neil," I said, "give Rory your weapons. Rory, hide them, then go back to your flock. You have seen no one. No one at all."

I gave the boy the Prince's pistol, and Neil handed over his broadsword, pistols and large dirk and took Rory's shepherd's crook; the boy hurried off.

"Now, sire," I said. "Walk behind me. Take small steps, keep your head down, and do not speak unless spoken to. What is your name?"

"Betty Burke," said the Prince; his Irish accent wasn't bad.

Chapter 14

As we made our way towards the coast, I saw a troop of Redcoats approaching. I hadn't seen these soldiers before, but knew from their tall mitre-like hats that they were Marines. We stood aside off the path to let them past, but the Colour-Sergeant eyed us suspiciously.

"Troop! Troop – Halt" he said. "Stand at – Ease! Now, Miss. Who are you? And what is your business here?"

"Why, sir," I said, "I am Miss Flora MacDonald of Milton. This is my maid, Betty Burke. And this is my man, Neil MacEachainn. We are on our way to Skye. Here is our passport."

I passed the laissez-passer to the Sergeant. He read it slowly, his lips following the words, and glanced at each of us in turn. The Marines weren't interested, and chatted amongst themselves. Neil relaxed, his hands resting on his crook. The Prince scratched his crotch unconsciously and the Sergeant caught the movement. So did I; I stepped forward and slapped "her" face hard.

"Stand still and show some respect for His Majesty's troops, you useless jade," I said. Betty lowered her head, rubbing her face. I turned to the Colour-Sergeant and gave him a winning smile.

"I sometimes wonder why I bother," I said. "Irish, of course."

"Well," he said, "that says it all, don't it? Here's your passport, Miss. A pleasant journey to you."

"Thank you, Sergeant. And good luck catching these Rebels."

"Don't you worry, miss. We'll root them out."

He turned to face his men, and called, "Troop! Troop – shun! By the front, quick – march!"

We watched the Redcoats march off. I glanced at the Prince, who was still rubbing his face; he looked at me with considerable respect. Neil didn't know where to look; but, needs must.

"Come on," I said. "We still have a good way to go." I set off at a good pace; I didn't want any discussion of my action, and to be quite honest my legs were trembling at the close encounter with the Marines.

As we made our way across the moor to the rendezvous cove, I assessed the situation in my head. I knew from Father that the British navy had sealed off the north and south entrances to the Minch, and patrolled it constantly, so there was no chance of a French ship slipping in there. So that meant the best chance of connecting with the French was either on Skye or Raasay, or an isolated spot on the mainland opposite. But we had to get off Uist as soon as possible, because the Redcoats plainly knew the Prince was somewhere on the Long Island, and we could not hope to fool every patrol as easily as the last one, especially as Himself was so thoughtless.

***

I thought that night would never end, but we had to keep going for we were due to rendezvous at dawn with the boat Neil had arranged. It was warm, and we were plagued with midges. Neil and I were used to them, of course, but they drove the Prince mad. Neil actually believed they were attracted to him because he drank so much brandy, and then sweated it out. In any event, Himself cursed and swore, jumped up and down, and waved stalks of bracken in front of his face in a vain effort to drive the midges away. All of these antics meant that he wasn't watching where he was going, and he fell several times in the boggy moor.

At one point, the Prince floundered across a marshy hollow, sank up to his knees in the mud, and his gown ballooned out like a huge flower. "Porco Madonna!" he said as he struggled to free himself. Neil hauled him out, but the Prince had lost one of his shoes. Neil took off his doublet, rolled up his shirt sleeve above the elbow, lay down on the mud and groped in the bog for the shoe. He stood up, spitting peat out of his mouth, and handed the shoe to the Prince who, without so much as a thank-you, banged out the mud, put it on, and set off again. As Neil rolled down his sleeve and put his doublet back on, he glanced at me; his grim look spoke volumes.

Chapter 15

Around midday, hours late, we reached the cove where the boat was hidden. It was a traditional double-ended Grimsay boat, clinker-built, about twenty-five feet in length, and deceptively strong. I knew that, for I had sailed in them many times between South Uist and Skye. This boat had a crew of four, and was skippered by Alan MacDonald. All were in the uniform of the Highland Militia. As we clambered aboard, one of the boatmen, John MacInnes, muttered in Gaelic to his mate, "Don't fancy yours!" His friend fell about shaking with silent laughter.

"Show some respect for your Prince, you idiots!" Neil snapped in Gaelic. The boatmen did a double-take as they darted a look at the maid and realised she was indeed a man, a tall man.

Just as Alan MacDonald was about to push off, I saw a cutter full of Redcoats approaching. "Look out!" I said.

The boatmen quickly fingered our boat back into cover behind the rocks as the cutter headed straight towards us, Captain Scott clearly visible in the stern. We all ducked down below the rocks and the cutter rowed straight past our hiding-place, the helmsman chanting, "In-out, in-out." It was just then that I noticed Neil holding a pistol to the back of the Prince's head; there was the faintest click as he cocked it slowly. I couldn't restrain a gasp. Neil heard it, scowled, shook his head, and put his finger to his lips, mouthing "sssh." Eventually the cutter vanished behind a headland and we all heaved a sigh of relief; Neil uncocked his pistol.

As the Prince scrambled into the boat, I grabbed Neil's arm and hissed, "What, what were you – ?"

"Flora," Neil whispered. "Between you and me, my orders are to kill the Prince rather than let him be taken alive."

I was speechless.

Alan said, "Hurry up."

Neil and I clambered into the boat, Alan pushed off, and said, "Give way – together." The boatmen rowed the boat in and out of the numerous skerries in the area as Alan kept a weather eye open; it was a flat calm. The Prince seemed in better spirits now, as there were no midges at sea, and hummed the Jacobite tune, 'The 29th of May.' I stared at Neil, hardly able to credit what he had just told me, but he appeared oblivious.

Occasional catspaws showed that a westerly breeze was building up, and they soon became regular. Alan said, "Ship your oars, and hoist the sail."

The boatmen hoisted the lugsail and the jib, the boat heeled over and picked up speed, and Alan put the tiller over so that we were heading due east towards Skye. Neil, the Prince and I exchanged a satisfied smile; so far, so good.

***

As night fell, the wind strengthened and a heavier sea was running, so Alan shortened sail. But our sturdy boat skimmed across the waves, making good speed. It was then I noticed something to windward.

"Look out!" I called. "A ship!"

A Royal Navy man-o'-war loomed out of the darkness, Alan went about into the wind, and we all instinctively crouched down. The ship hissed past us only fifty feet away. I caught a glimpse of Captain Scott on the quarter-deck as it vanished into the night.

***

When I woke later, dawn was breaking, there was a thick fog, and I found that my head was lying in the Prince's lap. His cloak was covering me, and he had made a cradle of his fingers over my head. He smiled at me, and said, "My Lady Flora, the crew were moving about during the night, and I wanted to protect your head."

I sat up, embarrassed, and said, "Thank you, sire."

It was an eerie atmosphere in that fog; it was flat calm, but you could barely see your hand in front of your face, and the sails hung loose.

"Sssh!" Alan said.

We all listened; nothing, except the slap of water against the hull.

"Where do think we are, Alan?" Neil said.

"We must be near Waternish," Alan said. "But I can't hear the breakers. Run out the oars. Give way – together!" The crew rowed the boat through the fog for several minutes.

"Oars!" Alan said. We drifted silently, everyone straining their ears. Somewhere close-by, a herring-gull screamed, and we all jumped.

"Give way – together!" Alan said. As the boat slid through the water, there was a puff of wind, and cliffs became visible.

"Ardmore Point," Alan said.

As we rounded the point, and were about thirty yards from the beach, a militiaman with a musket appeared. Alan put the tiller hard over, and said, "Row, my lads, row as if the devil himself was after you."

On the shore, the militiaman yelled, "Halt! You in the boat – halt! Come back here!"

"In, out. In, out. In, out," Alan said. "Come on, lads."

There was a bang! from the beach. I ducked. The musket ball whined past and gouged a big splinter out of the tiller beside Alan's hand. He barely paid attention to it. "Come on, lads, come on," he said.

Just then a file of MacLeod militiamen appeared on the beach, but by now the boat was fairly shifting, and with a few strokes we were out of range. The Prince laughed out loud and waved cheekily to the militiamen.

"A warm welcome to the Isle of Skye, eh, gentlemen?" he said.

Neil and I exchanged an astonished glance; to him, it was just a boy's game. But if that musket ball had hit him, it could have taken his head off.

***

We rounded Waternish Point and headed across Loch Snizort towards the Trotternish Peninsula. The fog had disappeared, and the sun was out. Shortly, we grounded on the beach near Monkstadt and a couple of the boatmen hauled the boat up on to the sand. Neil and I got out, the Prince made to follow, but I said, "Sire, stay here while Neil and I go to my kinsmen at Monkstadt and learn the lie of the land. Should anyone appear, let the boatman do the talking, and keep your head down. Alan, if a MacLeod militiaman comes over, explain that Betty Burke is my maid, and curse her for a lazy jade."

The Prince scowled, but nodded assent, while Alan suppressed a smile.

Chapter 16

I wasn't thinking when I walked right into the dining-room at the big house, so I was taken completely by surprise. Besides Lady Margaret MacDonald and her Factor, Alexander MacDonald of Kingsburgh, a Lieutenant of the Skye Militia was seated at the table. Fortunately he didn't see me immediately. But Lady Margaret did, and I could see she was about to panic. Kingsburgh noticed this, and cool as an autumn breeze, stood up.

"Why, Flora, my dear," he said. "What a pleasant surprise."

"How good to see you, uncle," I said; we kissed.

"Come," Kingsburgh said. "Let me introduce you to Lieutenant Alexander MacLeod of Balmeanach. Mr MacLeod – this is Flora MacDonald, daughter of Captain Hugh MacDonald of Armadale."

"A pleasure, Lieutenant," I said.

MacLeod stood up and bowed. "Miss MacDonald," he said. He was a shifty-eyed, suspicious little man; we shook hands.

I went round the table and hugged Lady Margaret. "Dear Lady Margaret."

"How lovely to see you, Flora," she said. I squeezed her arm tightly, trying to signal 'be calm' with my eyes. I turned to Kingsburgh, my eyes again flashing caution, and said, "Uncle Alexander, one of your tenants is outside wanting to see you. Something about the estate."

"Really?" he said. "Excuse me, I pray you."

As he went out, I sat down and Lady Margaret served me some lamb stew. I made myself eat slowly as Macleod watched me.

"So, Miss MacDonald," he said. "You've just come over from Uist?"

"That I have, Lieutenant. I am on my way to my mother's at Armadale and called in to pay my respects to Lady Margaret."

"And tell me, Miss MacDonald, what do they say about the Young Pretender in Uist?"

"The Young Pretender?" I said. "Why, sir, I do not think I take your meaning."

"There is much intelligence here that the son of the Pretender is skulking on Uist."

I laughed. "There are so many rumours about this person among silly people that quite frankly, sir, I pay little attention. I even heard that he was gone to St. Kilda."

"That much I heard myself," Lady Margaret said. Good for you, I thought, you've cottoned on quickly.

"The wretch is either dead or gone to France," I said. "This is quite capital lamb, Lieutenant, wouldn't you agree? I do believe I will have another spoonful, if you would be so good."

As MacLeod served me, I glanced out the window, and saw Kingsburgh and Neil walking up and down slowly, but I could see that their conversation was urgent. In the distance, at the gate, I could also see a couple of MacLeod's Militiamen sitting and smoking. How many of them were there?

As Lady Margaret poured more wine for MacLeod, the mincing little ninny tried his tricks again. "It is said, Miss MacDonald, that the Papists on South Uist and Barra are Jacobites to a man. Might they then not hide the Pretender?"

"Why, Lieutenant MacLeod," I said, "you surely do not expect me to speak for Papists? Who knows what they might think? And forbye, I do not think that they are as hot for the Pretender as you aver. Clanranald did not call his clan out after all. Is that not so, Lady Margaret?"

"Quite correct, my dear Flora," she said. "No more did my own chief, MacDonald of Sleat. Pray pass a potato, Lieutenant, if you would be so good."

"So where is your boat now, Miss MacDonald?" MacLeod said.

"Directly below the house, Lieutenant, on the beach. Some cheese?"

MacLeod made to stand up, saying, "No thank you, I had better – "

"Oh come, Mr MacLeod," I said. "The Trotternish cheese is famous. And you must fortify yourself against your arduous duties."

I cut a large piece and put it on his plate along with some oatcakes. Just then Kingsburgh came in and sized up the situation at a glance. He placed his hand on MacLeod's shoulder.

"Do excuse me, Lieutenant," he said. "Some pressing estate business. Now. You must have a dram with me before I return home."

He put the brandy decanter and two glasses on the table. I exchanged a quick glance with Lady Margaret and we prepared to withdraw. Kingsburgh caught my eyes and his own flicked towards the hill visible through the window.

"If you would collect your baggage from the boat, Flora, I will escort you on your way."

"Thank you, uncle," I said. "That would be a pleasure."

As I left, I permitted myself a secret smile; I felt rather pleased with myself for fending off MacLeod's probing. I was becoming quite good at this game.

Chapter 17

I arrived back at the boat to find the Prince sulking, staring out to sea, with the boatmen at a respectful distance. I gave him my bag, saying, "Now, sire, if you would carry this, it will add to the disguise."

He accepted it with an ill grace, and clumped off inland with his cutlery-canteen under his arm; he did not even say 'goodbye' to the boatmen let alone 'thank you'. I whispered to them in Gaelic that he was exhausted and had a lot on his mind, and thanked them profusely, but noticed Alan MacDonald and John MacInnes exchanging a 'that'll-be-right' look.

"I think you've got your hands full with Himself," Alan said. I gestured 'what-can-I-do?' and set off after the Prince while the crew prepared to run the boat into the water.

As we hurried along towards the hill which Kingsburgh had indicated, the Prince was still sulking and not paying attention to where he was going. It was lucky I spotted them.

"Down!" I hissed.

The Prince stood looking about stupidly, so I grabbed his arm and pulled him to the ground. He wrenched his arm away and was about to remonstrate when I jammed my hand over his mouth, and pointed. The two Macleod Militiamen were walking quickly towards the beach, their muskets slung.

"Hey, boatmen!" one of them yelled. "Wait there!"

But I heard him mutter to his mate, "It's a waste of time, innit? If the Pretender was on it, he'll be long gone." The mate said, "That's for sure."

I watched them engage Alan in conversation, then turned to the Prince. "Do you see that hill?"

"Yes."

"Neil is waiting for you behind that hill. Off you go, as fast as you can, and keep low."

I was so busy keeping an eye on the Militiamen that I didn't notice that the Prince had left his canteen behind on the machair. But whatever story Alan told them obviously worked, because the boatmen ran the boat into the water and set sail. I hurried back to the house, arriving just in time to see Kingsburgh and Lieutenant MacLeod finish their dram and prepare to leave. I took a couple of deep breaths and strolled in.

"I must be on my way," I said.

"Do give my love to your mother, Flora, my dear," Lady Margaret said. "And don't make it so long before we see you again."

"I promise, Lady Clanranald."

"And I must away to Kingsburgh," Uncle Alexander said. "I will ride with you on the road, Flora. Lady Clan. Mr MacLeod. Good day to you."

Lady Margaret handed Kingsburgh a package, with a knowing glance. "Some refreshments for the journey, Alexander."

"Thank you, Madam. You are too kind."

"Adieu, Flora," Lady Margaret said; I knew she meant it literally.

***

As Kingsburgh and I rode along the path towards the hill where Neil and the Prince were hiding, I reined in. Neil was running downhill at a breakneck speed towards the beach. What on earth was going on?

Urging my horse forward, we soon found the Prince. He was sitting on a rock, making no attempt whatsoever to conceal himself, throwing stones at the sheep ill-temperedly. As we rode up, he jumped to his feet and produced a cudgel from under his petticoat.

"Ah, Lady Flora," he said, "what – "

"What on earth is going on, sire?" I exclaimed. "What is Neil doing down on that beach?"

"He forgot to bring my canteen of cutlery," the Prince said in a petulant tone.

I raised my eyes to heaven, fuming. "Have you taken leave of your senses, sire? Are you entirely witless? Don't you know that the MacLeod Militia are down there? You saw them yourself, confound it all. You owe your life ten times over to that man, and yet you put his life in jeopardy for a box of trinkets!"

The Prince actually recoiled a couple of paces, while Kingsburgh muttered, "Flora, Flora," in a horrified tone. He nudged his horse forward a pace or two.

"Sire, sire," he said, "I am MacDonald of Kingsburgh, come to serve Your Highness."

The Prince ignored him completely. He stepped forward, drew himself up to his full height, looked up at me, and took a deep breath.

"Mademoiselle," he said. "For twenty years, I have had but one mission – the Cause. My whole destiny is to recover my father's kingdom for him. There is no other meaning to my life. When I led that small army south, and nearly, oh so nearly, took the whole country, it seemed that my destiny was about to be fulfilled. But thanks to weak-hearted and ignoble men who failed me, that purpose was thwarted, and my destiny remains unfulfilled. Having been reared entirely for this Cause, I have now failed. I have failed my father, I have failed myself, and I have failed my Highlanders. I am destroyed, Mademoiselle, do you see, destroyed utterly. If I have no grace left in my being, that is why. I must offer you my heartfelt apologies if I have offended you. And the same goes for the gallant and good MacEachainn."

The Prince was nearly in tears; if the truth be told, so was I.

"Sire," I said. "I beg you to convey these sentiments to Neil. He would understand. As I do."

As I wiped a tear from my eye, and Kingsburgh coughed with embarrassment, Neil jogged slowly up the hill with the canteen of cutlery under his arm. Breathing heavily, he handed the canteen to the Prince, and bent over, his hands on his knees. The Prince stowed the canteen in my bag, then stepped up to Neil, raised his head with his hands, and kissed him gently on both cheeks.

"My dear, good, true friend," he said. "Thank you. Thank you for all you have done for me since Culloden. I would be honoured to call you brother. When we return to France, I will repay my great debt to you, of that you can be sure."

Poor Neil! He didn't know where to look; he

touched his cheek in amazement, overcome with pride.

"Merci, monseigneur," he murmured.

The Prince turned round. "My dear Kingsburgh," he said, "it is my very great pleasure to meet you." They shook hands. The Prince then addressed me.

"My Lady Flora. You are the best Lieutenant I have ever had. I am utterly in your hands. I beg you to conduct me out of Skye to the mainland, where I may rendezvous with one of the French ships seeking for me. I must get back to France at once and return with a French Army."

"Sire," I said, "you may rely upon me to do that. But first we will go to Kingsburgh House to rest and refresh ourselves. You will be safe there."

Chapter 18

We pressed on towards Kingsburgh House, Alexander and I on horseback, the Prince and Neil on foot. I had lost track of time completely and only realised it was the Sabbath when I heard the sonorous sound of precenting psalm-singing as we approached a kirk. I turned to Neil.

"That is the last psalm before the blessing," I said. "And there is no cover here. We must try to pass before the people come out. Alexander, go ahead with the Prince. Neil and I will come behind. Quickly, now."

Alexander rode off at the trot, the Prince beside him, chatting away. Despite his disguise, he didn't look anything like a woman, to tell you the truth. In fact, he looked quite comical, with his great long strides. I was about to caution him when the doors of the kirk opened and the congregation streamed out, looking at us as we passed. Several of them I knew quite well, and we exchanged greetings; they would be wondering why I, a good Presbyterian, was travelling on the Lord's Day.

Just past the kirk, a stream ran down the hillside and across the road, perhaps a foot deep. To my horror, the Prince lifted his skirts knee high in front of him and plunged in. I could hear every word the locals said, in Gaelic.

"What an ill-shaped big lump of a woman," said

one old lady. "And very familiar with her master."

"Aye," said another. "And did you see the way she lifted her skirts? Shame on her!"

"And ugly as well as ungodly," said her husband.

"Probably a Papist then," said another. "Och, it's yourself, Flora. Good day to you."

"Good day," I said. Neil and I exchanged worried looks, but the Prince was oblivious to the comments and strode ahead, still holding his wet skirts high in front of him. I spurred my horse forward to catch up with him, with Neil jogging beside me.

"Sire," I said. "I am sensible to your lack of practice with your dress, but you must modify your gait. Your steps are far too great. And I beg you, do not lift your skirts so high when crossing a stream. The locals are commenting on it. And please take off your stockings and shoes when fording a stream. No local woman would keep them on to be soaked."

The Prince laughed. "Why, my dear Lady Flora, thank you for your solicitude."

"My solicitude is not just for you, sire," I snapped. "And it is no laughing matter."

I turned to Kingsburgh, who was looking very sheepish. "Alexander," I said. "I feel you would be safer taking Himself on the hill path, with Neil as rearguard. I know it is longer, but it would be safer. I will ride ahead, and wait for you at Kingsburgh House."

As Kingsburgh, Neil and the Prince set off up the hill, I urged my horse forward at the trot.

***

Night was falling as I approached Kingsburgh House. The breeze carried a faint song towards me. I reined in, and listened; there it was. Someone was singing "Greensleeves," a song no local would sing. I walked my horse forward carefully, and stopped in the shelter of a copse. A bonfire blazed in a field next to the big house, and I could hear the sound of English voices. Several Redcoats passed in front of the fire. I caught my breath, dismounted, and led my horse downhill quietly.

Passing behind the house, I led the horse into the courtyard; there was nobody about. I opened the stable door, which creaked loudly. I froze. But no one appeared. I led the horse inside and closed the door. Flitting across the courtyard, I tried the kitchen door. Locked. Just then, two Redcoats passed the entrance to the courtyard, talking in their revolting Cockney accent, and laughing. I froze again, but they carried on.

I could see a light at a first floor window, so I scooped up a handful of gravel and threw it up. It rattled loudly against the glass panes, and my heart jumped into my mouth. Nothing. So I scooped up another handful and tried again. The window groaned open, and thank the Lord, Anne MacAlister, Kingsburgh's daughter, looked out. "Who's there?" she said.

"Anne, sssh. It's me, Flora. Let me in."

"Flora? What the – ?"

"Quickly."

A moment later, the kitchen door opened, and Anne appeared with her mother, Florence MacDonald, in their nightgowns. I flitted inside and Anne threw the bolts.

"Why, Flora," Florence said, "what's going on? Why the secrecy?"

"Your husband is coming down on the hill path, with Neil MacEachainn of Howbeg, and a Jacobite fugitive. I must go to meet them and alert them to the presence of the Redcoats. In the meantime, could you prepare something to eat?"

"Of course."

A little later, I guided Kingsburgh, leading his horse, past the drinking and singing Redcoats. The Prince followed on tiptoe, and Neil brought up the rear, a cocked pistol in each hand. We crept into the courtyard, and Kingsburgh put his horse in the stable.

Anne and Florence, now dressed, were waiting in the kitchen. As the Prince entered, he bowed, and kissed Mrs MacDonald's hand. "Your servant, Madame," he said.

I could see from Florence's face that she knew the "maid" was a man. As Anne led the Prince and Neil into the dining-room, she turned to Kingsburgh and said, "And who is the fugitive in that ridiculous disguise, Alexander?"

"Why, it is the Prince, my dear," he said. "You have the honour to serve him in your own house."

Florence's jaw fell, and she gasped. "Oh my God! We shall be hanged if he is found here."

"Well, you can only die once," Kingsburgh said. "And if we are hanged, it will be a in a good cause."

"But I have no food fit for a Prince."

"My dear Florence, that man is so hungry, he would eat a horse."

Chapter 19

It was late when the Prince, Kingsburgh, Mrs MacDonald, Neil and I sat down to the table. A log fire blazed in the hearth and heated the room. Anne MacAlister served fried eggs, cold cuts of meat, cheese, bread and butter, then opened some bottles of beer and poured one for the Prince. He ate as if famished. Noticing Anne hovering, he said, "Madame, you are no servant. Pray be seated."

Embarrassed, Anne glanced at me for help.

"Sire," I said. "Mrs MacAlister is serving you for no servant must know you are in this house. The area is full of Redcoats and Militia."

"Ah," the Prince said. "I understand."

Later, the meal finished, Anne and Florence cleared the table, while Kingsburgh put out a brandy decanter, a china punchbowl, a silver ladle and a silver pot of hot water. The Prince sat in an armchair beside the fire, filled a pipe and lit it. Neil and I sat at a small table with a map of Skye, discussing in Gaelic the next move.

"Where is the most dangerous place in Skye?" I said.

"Portree," said Neil. "It's garrisoned."

"Exactly. They won't expect us there, so that's precisely where we should go. And from there, we should go over to our friends in Raasay who will get Himself to the mainland."

"Yes, I agree."

"The thing is, we have no intelligence of the whereabouts of – "

Just then, there was a barely audible tap-tap-tap at the French window; everyone froze. A moment later, the tapping resumed; someone was being very discreet. Quick as a flash, I pulled the Prince out of the armchair where he was sitting, pushed him into mine, tied on his bonnet, and dumped some knitting in his lap. As I sat opposite him, picking up some sewing, Neil dived into the armchair beside the fire, shoving a pistol under the cushion. He glanced round, and nodded to Alexander, who drew the curtain and peered out through the glass. There was nothing to be seen. It was very dark, with clouds scudding past the moon, creating ominous flashes of light and shadow.

Alexander unlocked the French windows and stepped outside. Ever so slowly, Neil cocked his pistol under the cushion. Alexander reappeared, looking puzzled.

"Neil," he said. "It's for you. A messenger."

Neil stood up, frowning, and went outside, pointing his pistol before him. I could hear his voice clearly.

"Who's there?" Neil said in Gaelic.

"Ici," said a voice from the darkness. Ah, it was a Frenchman.

"Qui etes-vous?" Neil said.

"Arretez-vous la," the voice said. There was the double click of a pistol being cocked.

The voice spoke again. "Pour le bonheur – ?"

"de la cause," Neil said. It sounded like a password.

"Lieutenant MacEachainn?" the voice said in French.

"Lui meme."

"Une lettre pour vous. Après l'avoir decodé, brûlez-la. Entendu?"

"Oui."

"Bonne chance, mon Lieutenant."

"Merci, camarade."

"A toute a l'heure."

"Au revoir."

I wished I could speak French, for I had no idea what they were saying, although it was obvious that it was important. Neil came back in, Alexander closed and locked the French windows, and drew the curtains. Neil drew his dirk and slit the envelope which was embossed with an official-looking wax seal. He turned to Kingsburgh.

"Alexander," he said. "Can I borrow your bible?"

"Certainly." He handed Neil the big family bible.

"Some paper and a pen, please."

Alexander fetched these. We all held our breath and watched as Neil turned from page to page, randomly, it seemed, decoding the message. It didn't take long. Neil looked up to find everyone staring at him.

"Alors?" said the Prince.

It wasn't difficult to work out what that meant.

"A French frigate is on its way to Loch nan Uamh for you, and will be there in a couple of days."

"Excellent news," said the Prince. "Excellent!"

"The bad news is that it's a long way to go in a couple of days," Neil murmured to me in Gaelic.

As Kingsburgh prepared the punch, Neil and I sat together and went over our options. The main problem was finding a boat to get over to Raasay from Portree, while avoiding Redcoat patrols. But I had a cousin twice removed who I thought might be able to help. It was around midnight when the Prince said, "Come and join us, my good Neil."

I could see that Himself was already tipsy, but was in the mood for more drink, so I bade the company goodnight. It had been a long and exhausting day.

Chapter 20

Anne had kindly given me her bedroom, so I lit the candles, took off my outer clothes and sat at the dressing-table in my sark to brush my hair. It was a Queen Anne dresser with 'batwing' mirrors, so I could see three reflections of myself. Anne MacAlister has good taste, I thought to myself; it must have cost a pretty penny.

I was so tired that I had difficulty keeping my eyes open as I brushed my hair. From downstairs, I could hear the faint sound of the men talking and laughing. The Prince's voice rose to a petulant level, and there was the snap of breaking crockery. The *drongaire*'s dropped the punchbowl, I thought. Shortly afterwards, slow footsteps dragged up the stairs, and staggered along the corridor. *Let's hope he's going to bed, and we can all get some sleep,* was my silent prayer.

The bedroom door crashed open, and the Prince lurched in. I froze, hairbrush in hand. He looked around, quite drunk, struggling to remove "Betty's" dress. It took a minute or two to get it off. Then he caught sight of me, or more correctly, the three reflections of me in the mirrors, my bare arms glowing in the candlelight.

"Mademoiselle," the Prince said. "I do apologishe. I appear to be in the wrong room."

He tried to focus, but was confused by the three images in the mirrors. At last he focussed on the middle one and took a step towards me.

"Why, my dear Lady Flora," he said. "You look absholutely ravishing."

He took another step towards me, his eyes fixed on the reflection of my breasts. "My dear, I had no idea you were quite so – "

I jumped to my feet and turned to face him, hairbrush ready, but my sark snagged on the stool, exposing my naked leg to the thigh. I was mortified. The Prince looked my leg up-and-down; he seemed very much less drunk now. Suddenly, he smiled. "Absholutely ravishing."

He lifted his hands as if to embrace me and took a pace forward, but I stepped smartly aside, and the Prince stumbled over the stool.

"Damn!" he said.

The anger in his tone seemed to unblock me. Just as I raised the hairbrush to thump the Prince, Neil appeared at the door. He took the situation in at a glance, seized the Prince and hustled him out of the room, his eyes signalling 'sorry' to me. I was fizzing with anger as I shut and locked the door.

***

The meeting in the kitchen next morning was stormy.

"Flora," Kingsburgh said in Gaelic, "I beg – "

"No," I said. "And no again. Under no circumstances will I have anything further to do with that despicable man."

"Oh dearie me," Mrs MacDonald said.

I stormed over to the window, folded my arms

and glowered at the pouring rain.

"The minute this wretched rain stops," I said, "I am off to Armadale. I should have been there days ago. My poor mother will be sick with worry."

As Kingsburgh and his wife exchanged despairing glances, Neil stepped up to me. He put his hands gently on my shoulders and said, "Dear Flora."

I screwed my eyes shut; I knew what he was going to say.

"Dear Flora," Neil said. "What the Prince did was unforgivable. It – "

"Unforgivable?" I said. "It was, it was monstrous. My father would kill him if he found out, Prince or no Prince."

"I know, Flora, I know. And he would be justified. It *was* monstrous. But it was a mistake. He was drunk."

"That's no excuse, Neil MacEachainn, and you know that fine well."

"I know it, Flora. But it helps understand it."

"Huh!"

"Flora. Please. A few more days. Just to Loch nan Uamh. We have exactly seventy-two hours to catch that French ship."

I clenched my teeth. "Under. No. Circumstances."

Neil patted my shoulder and moved away. None of us saw the Prince, dressed as Betty Burke, bonnet in hand, listening at the kitchen door. He couldn't understand the Gaelic, of course, but he would have understood my anger.

Neil tried again. "Flora. If you will not do it for the Prince, I beg of you to do it for me. I need you, Flora.

I do not know Skye, and I do not know the way to Loch nan Uamh. And you are well connected here. I beg you."

I was practically in tears; was there no limit to Neil's unswerving loyalty? He continued.

"Flora. For weeks now I have been skulking with Himself day and night, on ben and glen, never knowing where we were going to lay our head, never knowing what lay round the corner. It has not been easy. But, Flora. We have saved him so far. We must get him away to France. If we can only get him to Loch nan Uamh and onto that French frigate, he will be safe. Please, Flora. Please help me. Only three more days, then our task will be over."

He paused for a moment.

"Your father would expect that of you. For the good of the cause."

Tears were trickling down my face now. How could I resist such an appeal? For quite apart from the good of the cause, I knew now that I was in love with Neil. I wiped the tears from my eyes with the edge of my apron and turned to face him. Just then, the Prince stepped into the kitchen, startling us all. He turned to Kingsburgh and his wife, who were sitting at the kitchen table.

"I pray you good people to leave us," he said.

Kingsburgh and his wife left, looking very apprehensive, and shut the door behind them. I glared at the Prince. Neil muttered something in French which I didn't catch. The Prince stood there, eyes downcast, turning his bonnet over and over in his hand. He started to say something several times, but couldn't get it out. Eventually, he took a couple of paces forward, drew himself up to his full height, raised his eyes to meet mine and took a deep breath.

"Mademoiselle," he said.

"Yes?"

"Mademoiselle. I fear I have given you great offence."

"You have indeed, sir."

"I trust you will believe me, Mademoiselle, when I say that is something which I bitterly regret."

I said nothing. I could see that all this was very, very difficult for Himself. He had probably never had to apologise to anyone in his life. But I wasn't about to help him.

"I am singularly aware, Mademoiselle," he said, "of how much I owe to you."

He turned to look at Neil. "And to you, sir."

He turned back to face me. "I would rather die than give offence to you, Mademoiselle. I value your service beyond price. My only excuse is that I was drunk. And that is no excuse."

He took a very deep breath. "All I can do, Mademoiselle, is offer you my most abject apologies for my ungentlemanly conduct, and implore you to stay with me to Loch nan – "

He couldn't even pronounce it, and waved his hands helplessly.

"Uamh," I said.

"Uamh. Mademoiselle. I have need of you."

He bowed deeply. I looked over his back straight into Neil's eyes.

"Sir," I said. "I will come with you to Loch nan

Uamh. And further, if need be. That is my pledge."

Neil's eyes opened wide as he realised that I was addressing *him*, and a knowing smile flitted across his face. The Prince slowly raised his head, by which time I was looking at him again.

"Thank you. Mademoiselle. Thank you."

Chapter 21

Early the next morning, in pouring rain, Neil and I left for Portree; Himself would follow later in the day, guided by the shepherd boy MacQueen, one of Kingsburgh's people. Donald Roy MacDonald, a clansman who had been wounded at Culloden, had been sent ahead to find a boat for us. We would rendezvous with him at MacNab's Inn in Portree in the evening, and the Prince would be brought there. I arranged with Anne MacAlister to have Himself leave Kingsburgh House dressed as Betty Burke, but to change into men's clothes once well clear of the place. Fortunately, Anne's husband Ranald was about the same height as the Prince, so that didn't present a problem. I will pass over the details of that long ride, except to say that it was very wet, and by the time we arrived in Portree, the rain was torrential.

Near midnight, as we sat in the inn drying out, the boy MacQueen came in to say the Prince was waiting up the road; Neil and I went out to fetch him. The boy showed us where he was hiding under a tree on the other side of the roadside dyke, where there was a steep drop down to the sea. Just as we came up to Himself, I heard the sound of marching feet, and a squad of Redcoats appeared in the loom of the light from the inn coming towards us. Quick as a flash, Neil grabbed the Prince and shoved him to the ground.

"Keep down," he hissed.

Neil looked around desperately as the Redcoats approached. I seized his arm, backed up to the dyke, and pulled him into a clinch. Putting my arms round his neck, I closed my eyes and kissed him passionately. The Redcoats tramped past, whistling and yelling encouragement.

"Give 'er one for me, Jock," one shouted.

As they disappeared into the night, I realised that Neil was responding to my kiss, and he wasn't acting; that kiss was real. I opened my eyes. He opened his, and we stared at each other; I sank into his embrace, my heart thumping fit to burst. How hard and strong his body felt, I thought; I felt I would swoon. Just as Neil opened his mouth to say something, there was a rattle of stones from the other side of the dyke and the Prince whispered, "Have they gone?"

"Aye. Come quickly, for they may return," Neil said.

We took the Prince, who was drenched, down to the inn, where the first thing he wanted was a dram, which he downed in one. Donald Roy wanted to give him his dry shirt and kilt, but Himself would have none of it, saying that he would not take off his soaking wet clothes in front of a lady. Then we ordered some food, and MacNab brought us roasted fish, bread and cheese. We devoured this, and before I could say anything, the Prince paid for the meal with a golden guinea, saying he needed the change. Then the numbskull decided he wanted to change another guinea, but Neil told him that was foolhardy, for the innkeeper would surely be suspicious of someone flashing so much gold about.

Donald Roy insisted then that we leave, for the boat was due. As we made our way down to some boulders on the shore, mist rolled in from the sea. Donald Roy imitated the sound of an owl. In the distance, there was an answering hoot, and a small boat appeared. The Prince turned to me and said, "I do believe, Mademoiselle, that I owe you a crown of borrowed money."

"Sire, it is only a half-a-crown," I said.

"Here is a crown, Mademoiselle," the Prince said. Then he laughed. "It is all I possess."

He gave me a shiny new crown coin. Then he looked me in the eyes, and bending down, kissed my hand very gently. "For all that has happened, Mademoiselle, I hope that we shall yet meet in St. James's in London. Be sure that I will reward you there for all you have done."

The boat crunched onto the beach behind him. The Prince bowed again and stepped aboard. Neil squeezed my hand and was about to step into the boat too, when the Prince held out his hand to restrain him.

"You stay, my friend," Himself said.

The astonished Neil said, "Sire, my orders are – "

"*My* orders are that you stay here and convey my Lady Flora safely to her home," the Prince said.

"Sire, I – "

"Enough! Push off."

As Donald Roy pushed the boat off, the Prince said to Neil, "Tell nobody, not even my Lady Flora, which way I am gone, for it is right that my course should not be known. I will let you know by letter when I am clear. Au revoir, camarade."

As the boat vanished into the mist, a tear slid down my cheek, followed by another one. "He came in the mist, and he's gone in the mist," I said.

But as we turned to leave, I took comfort from the thought that I should have Neil's company for another couple of days.

Chapter 22

When we reached Armadale, my mother was surprised to see me, and asked why I had spent so little time with my step-father and brother on South Uist. But I told her I was upset by all the hustle and bustle the Redcoats were causing in the Islands, and did not feel safe there. Mother was quite satisfied with that explanation, and at no time did I tell her of my involvement with Himself. That would have been too much for her.

After a few days, a letter arrived for Donald Roy which he showed to Neil and me. It simply said:

Sir - I have parted (I thank God) as intended. Make my compliments to all those to whom I have given trouble.

I am, sir,
Your humble servant
James Thomson.

Donald explained that this was a code the Prince had arranged with him. It meant that the Prince was now safe with the Laird of Mackinnon in the south-west of Skye, who would convey him to the mainland and the rendezvous with the French ship.

There was a lot of commotion among the Skye Militia by now. I felt sure that they had learned that the Prince was on Skye. So it was no great surprise when I received a summons to go to Castleton to meet a lawyer who wanted to question me on behalf of MacLeod of Talisker. Both Neil and Donald argued that I should not go for it was obviously a trap. But I insisted I had to go, for to refuse would have been tantamount to an admission of guilt.

"Flora," Neil said. "To the English, what we have done is High Treason. Do you know what the penalty for Treason is?"

"No."

"Death. Death by hanging, drawing and quartering."

I gasped; the thought had never crossed my mind. "Be that as it may, I simply have to go to Castleton. If I don't go, they will know for certain I was involved with Himself."

Neil shook his head. But what we did do, however, was go over my story at length. And Neil took both the passport which my stepfather had written for me and the letter from the Prince to Donald Roy, and burned them. Such damning evidence could not be allowed to fall into the hands of the Redcoats.

The next day, I started for Castleton on horseback, while Neil set off to find the Prince and Donald took to the hills. On the road, I saw a party of Militiamen approaching. I was none too pleased to see it was commanded by Lieutenant Alexander MacLeod of Balmeanach, whom I had last seen at Monkstadt. The sneaking little gentleman actually smirked as he arrested me on the spot and took me off to HMS Furnace. My heart sank, for it was commanded by Royal Navy Captain Ferguson, whom we knew as the "Black Captain," a man whose reputation for cruelty was exceeded only by Captain Scott's. My heart sank even further on going on board to find that very same Captain Scott awaiting me.

"We meet again, Miss MacDonald," he said in a tone which chilled me to the marrow. I was locked in a tiny cabin, and shortly afterwards, the ship set sail. I couldn't stop my teeth from chattering, and my bowels turned to water; whatever my future was, it would be unpleasant. I sat down on the bunk before I swooned. It was imperative that I did not let Scott and Ferguson see that they terrified me.

Chapter 23

I brushed my hair, made myself as tidy as circumstances would permit, and composed myself; I had to, for the reputations of Captains Scott and Ferguson left me in a state of abject terror. There was the tramp of heavily booted feet, the door was opened, and there was the Royal Marines Colour-Sergeant I had encountered with Neil and "Betty Burke" on Uist, along with another Marine, both with muskets. His scowl showed that he remembered me only too well.

"Come along, miss," he said.

We marched along a passage-way on the lower deck and entered a spacious cabin; the stern windows were open and I could see we were anchored in Applecross Bay. The two Marines crashed to attention.

"Prisoner Miss MacDonald, sir," said the Colour-Sergeant. He and the other Marine took up position on either side of the door.

Behind a large table sat a gentleman in the uniform of an Army General, with Captain Scott on his right, Militia Lieutenant MacLeod beyond him, and Captain Ferguson on his left. At right angles to the table was a much smaller desk behind which sat a young Navy Midshipman with writing materials. Opposite, on another small table up against the bulkhead, was a silver tray containing a decanter of wine and several glasses.

"Good morning, Miss MacDonald," the General said. "Do you know who I am?"

"No, sir," I said.

"I am Major-General Campbell, Commanding Officer of all His Majesty's forces in Scotland."

Ah, I thought, that is good news. John Campbell of Mamore; at least he was a Highlander.

"I trust you are being well looked after?" the General said.

"Tolerably well, sir."

"Captain Scott," General Campbell said, "pray give Miss MacDonald a chair."

It was just as well the General did not see the scowl on Scott's face as he got up. It wasn't a chair he would have liked to give me. But I smiled sweetly, and said, "Thank you, Captain."

"Now, Miss MacDonald," said General Campbell, "do you know why you are here?"

"In truth, sir, I do not. But I am confident that you will make me sensible of your enquiries."

"Miss MacDonald. Our whole enquiry centres upon the present whereabouts of the Young Pretender."

"In these specifics, sir, I do not see how I can be of any assistance to you."

"Let us recapitulate your movements over the last couple of weeks, Miss MacDonald. Now…"

The interrogation lasted for more than two hours, accompanied by the scrinching of the Midshipman's pen, and the scowls and sneers of Scott, Ferguson and MacLeod, who plainly did not believe a word I was saying. But as I had rehearsed with Neil and Donald

Roy, I did tell the truth. Well, maybe not the *whole* truth, for by now Campbell would have intelligence that Betty Burke was indeed the Prince in disguise. Between them, Scott and Ferguson would have tricked or tortured the information out of the boatmen or servants, not to mention the local gentry, and I later found out that this was indeed the case. So I tried to protect my father by saying that I had asked him for the passport; I tried to protect Kingsburgh and his wife by saying that I had called at his house with the Prince and had sent for Donald Roy; and I tried to protect Neil by not mentioning him at all until I knew he was safe. And all the time I tried to remain calm and dignified, and to answer General Campbell's questions as honestly as circumstances would permit.

Eventually, it was nearly all over. General Campbell leaned back in his chair and said, "One last question, Miss MacDonald. All this time you knew that there was a price of thirty thousand pounds on the Pretender's head?"

"That consideration never even entered my mind, sir," I replied. "He was a fugitive on whom I took pity. To refuse assistance to a person in such a wretched state would have deeply offended our notions of Highland hospitality. I would even have offered a person with your surname hospitality, sir, were he *in extremis*. I am sure you will take my meaning."

General Campbell coloured, for he knew perfectly well I referred to the infamous massacre of Glencoe in the winter of 1692, when a company of Campbells was billeted on the MacDonalds of Glencoe and was received with open Highland hospitality. Then early on the morning of February 13th, the Campbells, on the order of the government, fell upon their hosts and murdered thirty-eight men, while a further forty women and children died of exposure in the winter snow trying to escape. The atrocity still blackened the name of Clan Campbell, and the General knew it.

I continued. "And to betray him having promised to assist would have offended my idea of honour. That, sir, is not allowable. Had I done so, I dare say Your Excellency would have looked upon me as a monster of a wretch."

Scott, Ferguson and MacLeod exchanged disgusted looks. But I noticed that Campbell was looking at me with something approaching admiration. Keep calm, girl, I thought.

"Thank you, Miss MacDonald," the General said. He turned to the Midshipman. "Do you have that, mister?"

"Aye, sir."

General Campbell turned back to me.

"You will be kept prisoner, Miss MacDonald, until your disposition is decided upon by higher authority. I will consign you to the custody of the Commodore of the Royal Navy flotilla in these waters on his arrival. In the meantime, although you are in a real scrape, I assure you that you will not be harmed. Do you understand?"

"Yes, sir." I made to stand, but the General put out his hand.

"Captain Scott," he said.

"Sir?"

"I would be obliged if you would pour Miss

MacDonald and me a glass of wine."

Scott stared at the General for a second, jaw open, but realised that he had just been given an order. He was choking with rage as he filled two glasses. He gave one to the General, who indicated that he should serve me first.

"Why, Captain Scott. You have been campaigning so long I do declare you have quite forgotten your manners."

Scott handed me the glass with a ghastly smile on his face; behind him, Ferguson and MacLeod looked equally outraged. The Midshipman could not believe his eyes.

"Slainte!" General Campbell said.

"Slainte mhor!" I replied.

We drank our wine without haste.

"Captain Ferguson," said the General.

"Sir?"

"As long as Miss MacDonald is detained on this vessel under your command, it is my express order that she be treated with respect, that she be treated like the honourable lady that she is. Otherwise, you will answer to me personally. Do I make myself clear?"

"Aye, aye, sir."

"Captain Scott. You are now relieved of all responsibility for Miss MacDonald. Is that clear?"

"Yes sir. Perfectly clear."

"Good. Mr MacLeod."

"Sir?"

"You may stand your men down. It is plain that wherever the Pretender is, he is not on Skye. Thanks to your efficiency."

"Very good, sir," said Macleod, squirming at the sarcasm. It took all my self-control not to burst out laughing.

"That will be all, gentlemen," the General said.

Scott, Ferguson and MacLeod left the cabin, their tails between their legs.

"Well, I fear your Prince has turned out to be a false prophet after all, Miss MacDonald," the General said.

"Not so much a false prophet, sir, more a prophet without honour in his own country." I looked down at my wine-glass, then back at the General. "The trouble is that I fear the prophet was the last hope for the Gaedhealtachdt."

"Well, Miss Flora, the fact of the matter is that very many Gaelic-speaking Highlanders and Islanders are actual or potential Jacobites, and therefore actual or potential Rebels. This the Hanoverians cannot tolerate."

"You are talking of many, many people, sir."

"My fear is that they will use this Rebellion as an excuse to rid the Highlands of many, many people."

I feared that the General was right. I put my wine-glass aside and stood up. "If that be the case, sir, then we both know that the Prince's cause was both noble, and necessary."

General Campbell stood up, forcing the gaping Midshipman to scramble to his feet too.

"Thank you for your indulgence, sir," I said.

"I wish you good fortune, Miss MacDonald."

"Thank you, General."

As I walked out, escorted by the two Marines, I heard the General say to the Midshipman, "Remarkable. A quite remarkable, clever woman, and a credit to Clan Donald."

Then he yelled, "And her father is a damned scoundrel, mister. A damned clever Highland scoundrel. Ha! Damn them all! They don't know it yet, but their days are numbered."

Chapter 24

I will pass over the next few weeks except to say that they were tedious. I was kept apart from the other prisoners, who now included Kingsburgh, presumably so that we could not agree our stories. But I was quite sure by now that the Hanoverians knew most of the details of the Prince's escape from Uist to Skye and onwards, and who was involved. What I was dreading was being taken to London, for the news of our people being hung, drawn and quartered there had reached Scotland. And I had no idea of what had happened to the Prince, although I had deduced he must have reached the mainland by now. Had he been captured on Skye, the Redcoats and the local Militia would have been crowing about it, but although there was still a lot of commotion, there was no news of Himself having been taken.

The Royal Navy Commodore allowed me to go home to say goodbye to my mother, but we were forbidden to speak Gaelic. On my return, I was accompanied by her maid, Kate MacDonald, who was to prove a loyal and welcome companion. Then I was held for a few days in Dunstaffnage Castle, before being transferred to HMS Eltham, which set sail for Edinburgh round the north of Scotland. We arrived at Leith on September 16th, 1746, where I was transferred to yet another ship, HMS Bridgewater. Little did I know that I was to remain aboard her for two whole months. But I was happy to see the back of Captain Ferguson.

On the whole I was well treated on this ship, although the boredom was oppressive, for I was not allowed ashore, not even to visit Kingsburgh who was held in Edinburgh Castle. However, I was allowed visitors, and a procession of Jacobite ladies came to see me; chief among them was Lady Bruce. To tell you the truth, I could have done without them, for their heads were full of the most awful nonsense about Himself. One of them, Lady Mary Cochrane, was stranded on board when a sudden gale blew up. She told me that it would be an honour to share the bed of the person who had been the Prince's guardian; what a silly woman!

But there was no news of the Prince at all, and the Jacobite ladies and I feared he had been captured. Then on October 27th, we set sail for London, where I expected to face trial, a prospect which alarmed me. But when we arrived there, I was taken to a Messenger-at-Arms' house where I found Clanranald, Boisdale and half-a-dozen other prisoners from the Hebrides under a form of open arrest. So at least I had the company of my own people. But the Hanoverians were still executing Jacobite Rebels, and in April of 1747, they even beheaded Lord Lovat. So I feared constantly for my fate, although there was still no news of a trial. But I derived much satisfaction from the news which eventually filtered through to us that the Prince had reached France along with Neil, and my stepfather was still free, hiding on Skye where no one would betray him.

Just as in Edinburgh, the Jacobite ladies of London – Lady Primrose in particular – made much of me, and raised a fund of £1,500 to help pay for my lodgings and legal expenses in the case of a trial. My portrait was painted, and several fanciful accounts of my involvement with the Prince were published. But to be quite honest, I could never understand why I was the subject of such a fuss.

However, can you imagine my surprise when one day that summer, it was announced that two gentlemen had come to visit me? One of them was Frederick, Prince of Wales, the son of the King and older brother of that despicable butcher, the Duke of Cumberland! Prince Frederick was very polite and charming, and asked me why I had aided Prince Charles to escape. I replied that it had been a matter of simple humanity, that the Prince had been in a miserable condition and starving, so I had agreed to take him across the water to Skye, and on to Portree.

"I am neither sorry for it, nor ashamed of having done so," I said. "If your Highness or any of your family had come to me under similar distressing circumstances, I would, with the help of God, have done the same."

I don't know if Prince Frederick had anything to do with it, but in July 1747, the Hanoverians passed the Act of Indemnity, which declared an amnesty for many Jacobite prisoners. I was released, stayed with Lady Primrose for a few days, then set off for Edinburgh in a post-chaise, arriving there on August 2nd.

William Dick's House
59 The Strand
London

Saturday July 4th, 1747

Dear Mother

I have heard today that I am to be released in a few days under the terms of the Act of Indemnity which has granted myself and many of the other prisoners an amnesty.

I will stay in London for a few days with Lady Primrose who has most generously raised a petition on my behalf, then travel north by post-chaise with Captain Malcolm MacLeod of Brea as my chaperone. As there is still a great deal of ill-feeling in England against the Scotch Highlanders, we intend to travel as brother and sister, a Mr and Miss Robertson. Captain MacLeod is a most trustworthy and honourable man.

Once we have reached Edinburgh, I intend to rest for a while, for it is a long and fatiguing journey, and I do not like the intelligence I am hearing about the attitude of certain parties in Uist and Skye towards me. Once the commotion has died down, as it will, I shall return to Armadale post haste.

Rest assured, dear mother, that I am in good health and spirits.

Your affectionate daughter,
Flora

The Scotsman's Courier

August 2nd, 1747.

The COURIER has learned that Miss Flora MacDonald and Captain Malcolm MacLeod of Brea have arrived in Edinburgh today on the post-chaise from London. Readers will hardly need reminding that Miss MacDonald is the lady who gallantly assisted the Young Pretender on his escape from South Uist to Skye, enduring many hardships and tribulations in the process. Miss MacDonald was arrested with many others from the Long Island; conveyed in a ship of the Royal Navy to the Leith Roads; imprisoned on HMS Bridgewater for many weeks; then conveyed to London where it was feared she would stand trial for High Treason; and suffer the melancholy fate of so many who supported the Stuart Prince on his ill-considered misadventure. However, the recent Act of Indemnity granted an Amnesty to Miss MacDonald, as well as Captain MacLeod and many of the other Jacobite prisoners.

We understand that Miss MacDonald will repose in Edinburgh for some time before continuing her journey to the Outer Hebrides.

Chapter 25

Early the next year, as I watched a company of kilted Highland soldiers march down Edinburgh's High Street, I reflected on the irony that the kilt was now forbidden in Scotland except for soldiers in the British Army. I had decided to stay in the city for a while, for if the truth be told, I was not keen to return to the Hebrides just yet. My brain was still whirling with the events of the previous year, and I wanted it to settle down before going home. Further, my step-father was still in hiding, and I had heard that some people in Skye and Uist were not well disposed towards me because of the leniency of my treatment. Given what might have happened to me in London, I was not well pleased with that news.

When the soldiers had passed, I crossed the street towards my lodgings in the Old Town, and noticed a beggar shuffling along the pavement. He was a bowed, unshaven, elderly man wearing a black eye-patch and shabby clothes, his coat collar turned up and his face shaded by a three-cornered hat. Probably an old soldier with no job, I thought.

I climbed the lighthouse stair to my house, and just as I opened the door, the beggar appeared behind me, pushed me inside, dived in after me and slammed the door. As I opened my mouth to scream for help, he whipped off his hat and eye-patch. It was Neil!

"Oh, Neil," I cried. We hugged and hugged.

I gave Neil a dram, and he told me all his news. He had connected with the Prince on the mainland shortly after my arrest, had endured numerous hair-breadth escapes from the Redcoats, and shortly afterwards they had been picked up by a French ship from Loch nan Uamh.

"When we reached France," Neil said, "Himself went about his business, and I was commissioned a Lieutenant in Albany's Regiment. But I continue to serve the Cause, which is why I'm back in –"

"Och, Neil," I said. "Have you any idea of the blood shed in the name of the Cause? The Cause? The Cause is finished, man."

"I can't agree with that, Flora. The French are thinking of sending an Army next Spring."

I laughed out loud. "A French Army? Now where have I heard that before? Neil, the French are just using us as pawns in their war-games with the English."

"We must never give up hope for the Cause. Between thee and me, I am on my way north to Badenoch to take soundings. Cluny MacPherson is still free, after all."

I sighed; you could do nothing with such a devoted man.

"I must go, Flora," he said. "I have a long journey north."

"And then you will return to France?" I said, hoping against hope.

"Yes. That is my duty. For the good of the Cause."

"I will stay in Scotland. In Skye."

We stood up. We both knew that there was nothing

else which could be said. So we kissed, with a great deal of affection. Then Neil resumed his disguise.

"Beannachd leat, a' Floraidh."

"Beannachd leat, a' Niall."

Epilogue

And that was that. I never saw Neil MacEachainn again, although I did hear he had managed to get back safely to France at the end of his mission up north. I always prayed he found happiness in France, and Himself rewarded him handsomely, for Neil had saved his royal bacon on more occasions than I could count. He was a fine, brave, loyal, clever man.

My stepfather, Captain Hugh MacDonald, came down from the hills when the hue and cry was over, and emigrated to America when my mother died.

Himself? I never heard a word from Prince Charles Edward Stuart again in my life. Not a letter, not even a message. He didn't care about us, you see. All he really cared about was his father's throne. And he would do anything to get that, anything, even if it meant destroying our way of life in the Highlands and Islands of Scotland. And he achieved that alright. To tell you the honest truth, *Is e mac na galla a tha ann,* as we say.

Myself? Well, I eventually did go back to Skye, and after some time married Allan MacDonald. We had five sons and two daughters. Allan was a good man, but he had no head for business, and conditions in the islands were deteriorating anyway. So in the summer of 1774, when I was fifty-two years of age, we too migrated to North Carolina, where so many of our people now live. We thought it would be the land of milk and honey, but it turned out to be a disaster for us, with a second Culloden. But that is another story…

THE END

Acknowledgements

Many thanks to Birlinn Press for permission to reproduce the translation of the Gaelic song *Tha mi am chadal, na duisgibh mi,* from Anne Lorne Gillies's *Songs of Gaelic Scotland* (2005.)

I am also very grateful to Murdo MacKay of Sheigra, Sutherland, for all his careful assistance with Gaelic words and phrases: Tapadh leat! I would also like to thank John MacKinven, my friend and fellow-student on the 2006 Master's degree in Creative Writing at the University of Auckland, New Zealand, for endless encouragement and helpful suggestions.